Andy Norman was born in South London and hasn't strayed far since. His upbringing and career have introduced him to some of the more Bohemian elements of South London life.

He currently plies his trade as a publican and *The London Lottery War* is his first novel.

This book is dedicated to my parents, who always believed in me but, unfortunately, are not with me to celebrate the publishing of my first novel.

Andy Norman

THE LONDON LOTTERY WAR

AUSTIN MACAULEY PUBLISHERS™

LONDON ★ CAMBRIDGE ★ NEW YORK ★ SHARJAH

A CIP catalogue record for this title is available from the British Library.

ISBN 9781785548581 (Paperback)
ISBN 9781786120229 (ePub e-book)

www.austinmacauley.com

First Published (2021)
Austin Macauley Publishers Ltd
25 Canada Square
Canary Wharf
London
E14 5LQ

To my family and friends who have provided invaluable encouragement and assistance in making this novel a reality. I salute you all.

Chapter 1

Friday, 28 October, 3:45 pm

It was a cold autumnal afternoon as James left work for the fifteen-minute drive home. It was the same tedious drive, getting caught at the same tedious traffic lights, the same tedious drivers not wanting to give an inch to any other car. All frightened that their journey may last an extra few seconds if they were to give way to another vehicle. James listened to a debate about immigration on Radio 5Live as he travelled. His mind drifting from the journey – one that he was convinced he could do blindfold as he had done so many times before.

James was 27 years old and worked as a machinist in a local steel fabrication workshop. Brought up in a suburb of South London, James had known some rough times as a kid. His father was a market trader, and although he made some money doing that, any real money he made James always suspected came from more nefarious sources. His mother kept them going, working as a cleaner in the morning and in the kitchen of the local primary school at lunchtime. Despite money being tight, they were a reasonably happy family. His older brother, Robert, had left home at the age of sixteen and rarely contacted the family.

***

Robert was a happy, contented five-year-old, enjoying his first year at primary school when he noticed that his mother was getting fat. This first came to his attention when he realised there was no room for him to sit on her lap. As his mother got bigger, she seemed to be sleeping more, and he was left in his father's care, which he did not appreciate. He had never been particularly close to his father, and as much as he tried, he could not have the same feelings for this large and rather grumpy man as he had for his loving and caring mother. Whilst his friends' fathers took them to the park to play football or even take them to watch the local football team to play on a Saturday, his father only ever took him to work with him or sat him in the corner of the local pub whilst he drank with his mates.

It was a Tuesday afternoon as Robert left his classroom and sprinted across the school playground and out of the gate. He turned to the right, his eyes darting around looking for his mother who was always there to greet him, but he couldn't see her. He stopped with a confused look on his little face and felt tears starting to well up in his eyes. She had not been waiting for him outside the school. He looked around, starting to feel a surge of panic coarse through him when he heard a voice. "Robert, Robert!" the voice called. He turned to see the smiling face of his Aunt Grace. He approached his aunt slowly and looking quizzical exclaimed, "Where's mummy, is she OK?"

His aunt smiled at him, "Mum's fine," she answered. "She's at home with a big surprise for you."

They walked home with Robert asking his aunt all the way what the surprise was. "You wait and see," was all she would tell him.

They reached the front door and before he could press the bell, the door was opened by his grandmother who picked him up in a huge bear hug and kissed him all over his face.

"Where's Mummy?" Robert asked as his grandmother carried him into the house.

"She's in the front room," she replied, carrying him to the door. "You must be very quiet."

He peered around the door and saw his mother sitting in the big high-winged armchair that his father usually occupied and cradled in her arms was what looked like a bundle of blankets. He tentatively approached the chair and heard a slight gurgling sound. His mother turned her face and smiled at him.

"Come and meet your little brother," she said, still smiling. "This is James," she told him.

Robert curiously peeked into the bundle of blankets and saw the tiniest and cutest little boy he had ever seen.

"James," she said, "this is your big brother Robert, he will always be around to look after you."

Robert felt the proudest he ever had in his so far short life and vowed to himself that he would never let this little boy down.

Over the coming months, James seemed to take up more and more of his mother's time, and Robert was once again left in the care of his father.

His father worked in various markets around London, and Robert started to enjoy these days out, not because he was with his father, but due to the other characters he would meet. Once he found his feet and his confidence, he would wander the length of the market talking to all the stallholders and running errands for some of them for which he would receive a handful of change as remuneration. He had an arrangement with the tea stall whereby he would remove the rubbish for them, and they would let him have a few cups of tea free of charge. This would come in handy as the stallholders would give him money to get them tea which he would get for free and keep the money. Robert was learning his first lessons in profit and gain, which he would continue to learn for the rest of his life.

By the age of ten, Robert was no longer accompanying his father to the market but instead going on his own. He had assessed that of all the markets they attended, East Street market was the most viable for him so he would be there every Saturday and Sunday morning and throughout the school holidays.

By this time little James was attending the same school, and Robert was constantly watching out for him. He would stand well away from James and his new friends and would only intervene if he saw something happening that he didn't like the look of.

"You'll make that boy soft," his father used to tell him every time he heard of Robert fighting another of James battles.

James would get up early every Saturday and Sunday morning and have breakfast with his brother before he went to the market and would sit enthralled listening to the stories about all the different characters Robert met there. He begged his mother to let him go with Robert, but she wouldn't hear of it. "When you're older," she would tell him.

James finally got his wish when he was nine. With Robert now 14 and bigger than most 16-year-olds his father told him he could take James and try and harden him up a bit.

James was fascinated by the people that Robert knew in the market. Most of them were obviously rogues and very hard men, but they seemed to accept Robert as one of their own and paid him handsomely to carry out various errands. Robert had moved on from fetching cups of tea and disposing of peoples' rubbish. James noticed lots of envelopes and cash changing hands.

As they walked through the market, Robert was stopping and shaking hands and talking to various stallholders when James heard a voice call out.

"Robbie!" a man called out in a rather gruff South London accent.

Robert turned around and saw the man beckoning him. He walked towards the man with James following behind.

Robert shook hands with the man, and the man whispered in his ear whilst giving James a rather suspicious look.

"This is my brother James," he said, and the man just nodded in his direction before turning his back on him. He turned his back on James and putting his arm around Robert's shoulders; he continued to whisper in his ear. When he finished talking to Robert, he looked around before removing an envelope from his inside pocket and handed it to him. Robert placed the envelope in his pocket.

"Stay here," he told James. "I'll be five minutes," he said as he turned to walk away.

James didn't like the look of the stallholder, and as soon as he turned his back, he shot off in pursuit of his brother. He could see him about fifty yards ahead of him. Disappearing in and out of the crowd, James was having trouble keeping track of Robert. He saw him shoot around the corner at the end of the street and increased his pace so as not to lose him. As James turned the corner, he heard Robert shouting.

"Let go of me!" he could hear him shouting, and as he got closer, he could see a policeman with a tight grip on Robert's sleeve.

James didn't know what was in the envelope that his brother was carrying, but he was pretty sure that Robert wouldn't want the policeman to find it. Breathing heavily James leant against the wall, his mind rushing to work out what he could do. Suddenly he grabbed at the collar of his sweater and pulled down with all his strength. He felt the material tear apart and reveal the vest that his mother had made him wear. Forcing himself to cry, he ran towards his brother, now firmly in the hands of the policeman.

"Help me, help!" he shouted at the top of his voice.

The policeman turned his attention towards the dishevelled little boy running towards him crying, still holding onto Robert he called out, "What's happened?"

"Three boys just beat me up and stole my money," James replied.

"Where did they go?"

"They ran off down the alley along the side of that pub," he told the policeman.

"Wait here," he told James, "and you," he said, turning to Robert. The policeman ran towards the alleyway whilst speaking into his radio.

As soon as he was out of site, Robert turned to James. "What happened?" he asked.

"Nothing," James replied, "I just needed to get you away from that copper."

Robert looked in amazement at his little brother and grinned at him from cheek-to-cheek.

"We'd best get out of here a bit sharpish," he told his little brother, laughing as he spoke.

They ran for another hundred yards and then ducked into a pub where Robert handed over the envelope to a man at the bar and he, in turn, handed Robert a wad of notes.

They looked right and left as they exited the pub and could see the policeman nowhere. They ran all the way back to the other end of the market via the backstreets and alleyways that Robert had come to know well over the years. When they finally reached the stallholder who had given Robert the envelope, they were both out of breath and still laughing.

"What's the matter with you two?" he asked.

Robert told the story of the policeman and James' rescue. The man very nearly smiled but instead just shook his head. Robert handed over the money the man in the pub had given him, and in return, the stallholder pulled a few notes off the roll and gave them back to Robert. As they started to leave the man looked over to James and beckoned with his head for the young boy to come closer. Putting his hand into the money pocket, he wore around his waist, he pulled out a small wad of notes and removed a tenner.

"That's for your quick-thinking young man," he said, passing the note to James.

He turned to his brother with a huge grin on his face. James had never had a £10 note of his own.

Robert smiled back at him "Let's get out of here before that copper comes back," he said.

The pair of them disappeared into the backstreets and ran for the next ten minutes until Robert was satisfied, they were far enough away from the, no doubt, seething policeman.

"Can I come with you again?" James asked as they walked back towards their home.

"Course you can," he said, "don't know what I'd do without you."

The pair of them started to laugh again.

From that day on they spent every weekend and all the school holidays together. James learned how to make a couple of quid, but Robert always took the lion's share explaining to his younger brother that one day he too could find his own apprentice and then he could be the boss. James had no aspirations in that area, he was just happy being with his big brother.

It was the day after Robert's sixteenth birthday that everything changed.

It was about nine o'clock on a Friday evening, and James was sitting watching TV with his mum when he heard the front door slam. His father staggered along the hallway and appeared at the living room door with a silly smile on his face. "All right, my darling," he slurred to his long-suffering wife.

Without averting her gaze from the TV, she said, "Your dinner is in the oven."

"I don't want dinner," he told her, "I need some money."

James saw the look on his mother's face. "Where are your wages?" she asked calmly.

"Don't worry about that," he replied, "just give me some fucking money."

James's mother rose from the corner of the sofa where she always sat and approached the pathetic looking man standing in the doorway.

"You've lost it playing cards again, haven't you?" she shouted.

"Give me some money!" he shouted again, this time getting louder.

"Give me my housekeeping," she shouted back at him.

His dad looked up the stairs at Robert, who had left his room and was now staring at his father, whom he loathed for the way he treated their mother.

"Robert," the drunk said, "you've got money, give me some!" he demanded.

Robert laughed at his father, "What, so you can drink more and throw it away in a game of cards!"

"Watch your mouth," his father shouted at him.

"You're pathetic," Robert said. "A drunk who can't even care for his own family," he continued as he moved closer to his father.

The old man took a swing at Robert which he easily evaded, and as he did so, his mother put herself between the two of them. He threw a second punch which completely missed Robert but caught his wife square on the jaw. The woman fell to the floor instantly. For a moment, the whole scene seemed suspended in time. Suddenly Robert exploded. A flurry of punches directed at his father all landed with precision-like accuracy knocking him to the floor. As Robert attempted to continue the violent attack his mother started screaming, trying to pull her eldest son away from the bleeding mess that was whimpering on the floor.

James just looked on in horror and could feel the tears welling up in his eyes. Robert got away from his mother's grip and turned towards the stairs. He climbed the first two steps before stopping and putting his hand into his pocket. He pulled out two £20 notes and threw them on the floor next to the crushed body of his father.

"Take that and fuck off you no good wanker!" he shouted as he climbed the stairs to his bedroom and slammed the door behind him.

James's mother helped her husband to his feet and tried to wipe the blood from his face.

"Leave me alone, woman!" he shouted as he bent down to pick up the money. "Tell him he better be out of my house by the time I get back." The door slammed behind him, and James and his mother just looked at each other in shock. She burst into tears and ran up the stairs to her bedroom, leaving James alone. He sat on the bottom stair and started to cry. After a minute or so, he heard a door open upstairs and footsteps descending the stairs towards him.

"Are you OK, James?" Robert asked.

James quickly tried to hide the tears that were now running down his cheeks.

"I'm fine," he lied.

Robert sat down on the stair next to his younger brother.

"I'm sorry about that, but it had to be done. Dad has been beating Mum for years and getting away with it, and I always knew that one day I would have to retaliate."

"I'm glad you did it," James replied, "but what will happen now?"

"Unfortunately, I am going to have to leave," Robert told him.

Robert's words hit James like a sledgehammer.

"What!" he exclaimed.

"I always knew this day would come," Robert told him. "I also knew that when it did happen, I would have to leave or he would make Mum's life even worse."

"Where will you go?" James asked.

"Don't worry about that," he told him. "I've got plenty of places I can go, but I don't want Dad to know where I am."

"I won't tell him," James said.

"You won't be able to James because I'm not telling you, it's safer that way," Robert stood up and climbed the stairs back to his bedroom leaving James to wonder what had happened to his life in the past fifteen minutes.

He could hear Robert moving around upstairs, drawers opening and closing and furniture moving. It went quiet for a few minutes, and then the door opened, and Robert appeared carrying a large holdall. He walked slowly down the stairs, and James stood at the bottom, waiting for his brother.

They stood face-to-face for a moment before Robert dropped his bag and pulled his little brother into a strong embrace. "I've left an envelope under the pillow in my room for Mum, make sure she finds it before Dad does," he whispered into James ear.

They parted from their embrace and stood silently, looking at each other for a moment. Robert then picked up his bag with one hand, and with the other, he produced an envelope from his inside pocket.

"Open that when I've gone," he said.

With that, he turned, opened the front door and left.

James slumped back onto the step and cried. Within one minute, his mother was sitting with him, also crying.

He told his mother about the envelope that Robert had left and then made his way to his bedroom. He lay on his bed and looked at the envelope that his brother had given him. He peeled it open and looked at the contents. It contained five £20 notes and a letter. The money went straight under the mattress and would remain there until he could find a better hiding place. He then opened the letter:

Dear James,

As I explained, I can no longer live under the same roof as that disgraceful character we know as our father. I have plenty of friends who will put me up until I get on my feet and I have plenty of money to keep me going. Be careful with the money I have given you and do not let Dad get his hands on it. I have given Mum some money to keep her going until he finally starts paying the bills and upkeep of the family.

Although I have no intention of returning, you can be assured that I will be thinking of you always. Through my network of friends, I will always know what's going on in your life and, one way or another, I will always be in the background to lend a helping hand.

I know I will regret leaving you and Mum and, for this reason, I will make this promise to you. If you are ever in any trouble or need my assistance in any way, I will know, and I will contact you and resolve your problems in any way I can.

Thinking of you always.
Robert
PS I will speak to the guys in the market and tell them to pass everything on to you.

James never went to the market again, and the only time he had seen Robert was five years ago at their father's funeral.

Chapter 2

As a single man, he only really had himself to consider when it came to where and how he spent his time and money, and most of both was spent in the local pubs. He'd never considered marriage despite having had a five-year relationship with a young lady that fizzled out due, in her words, to his lack of 'ambition and commitment'. He couldn't really deny either as his desire for a peaceful and relaxed life outweighed the responsibility of striving for the top and making fortunes. At 6ft tall with a chiselled torso and boyish good looks, he had no real problem in attracting the ladies but showed very little interest in relationships. James was a man who was relatively happy with the hand he had been dealt with. The only thing he yearned for that he didn't have was Lisa. She was his flatmate and best friend, and it appeared that that was all she would ever be, sadly.

Indicating to turn right, James waited patiently for the oncoming traffic to clear and then pulled into his street. As he did so, a car pulled out from the kerb directly outside his home. *What a touch,* he thought to himself as he pulled into the now vacant parking space and after releasing his seat belt, he exited the vehicle and pressed the button on his key fob to lock it.

Walking to the front door, he let himself in and went straight to the kitchen. He could hear the sound of music coming from the living room. It wasn't like any music he would be playing and was certainly a few decibels louder than he would have liked.

He opened the living room door and put his head around to see Lisa laying on the sofa eyes closed and humming away to the music. James and Lisa shared the two-bedroom maisonette and had done for over two years. It was a handy arrangement for them both and halved the rent.

"Afternoon," he called to her. Lisa turned her head and smiled, keeping her eyes closed. "No work today?" James enquired.

"James, it's Friday," she exclaimed, laughing, "you know I don't go to work on Fridays if I can help it."

"All right for some," he replied. "I'm getting washed and changed and then out for a pint. What you up to?" he inquired.

"May very well join you later," she replied. "I need to bath and make myself look lovely first."

Lisa loved life. She considered her life to be pretty good. She worked for a telesales company where every month she was in the top three for sales and therefore, commission. This success meant she could take real liberties with her company and more or less pick and choose her work hours. She made reasonable money but, as her boss told her, she could be amongst the real top earners if she applied herself better. Money was no huge incentive to her as, although she was only 24 years old, both of her parents had passed away. Her father when she was eight, although she never really knew him and her mother two years ago. As an only child, Lisa had been left quite a reasonable sum of money by her mother, which helped to make her life a bit more comfortable. She'd thought on numerous occasions about investing in a property for herself, but that would mean leaving James on his own, and she wasn't sure if she had the heart to do that. She was a very attractive young lady in a classical rather than pretty sense her shoulder-length auburn hair, usually tied in a ponytail was always neat and tidy, and she had extremely attractive dark brown eyes. At 5'4", she was not the tallest of women but was very nicely proportioned. Unfortunately, her hard-headed and some might say slightly arrogant ways had seemed to frighten most men away although this never seemed to bother her. She was very fond of James and often thought that things could go further but was completely unaware of what his feelings for her might be.

***

After a quick shower and shave James dressed, casual as always, nice jeans and a moderately expensive shirt, picked up his phone and wallet and headed towards the front door. "See you later," James shouted to Lisa as he passed the living room and without waiting for a reply opened the front door and left.

It was a five-minute walk that he did most evenings about this time passing the same houses the same parked cars and often the same people.

"Evening Jim," a man walking a huge Rottweiler called out from the other side of the street.

"Hi, Terry," James called back. "You out for a pint later?" He enquired.

"Yes mate, dropping Bruce home, and then I'll be down. Get one in for me," Terry replied, laughing.

James smiled and inwardly laughed to himself. Not so much because of what Terry said, but as to why people have suddenly decided to give their dogs human names. *Can't wait for someone to christen their baby Rover,* he thought to himself.

As he continued along, he suddenly noticed an envelope on the ground ahead of him partially hidden by an overgrown bush from someone's garden. As he got closer, it started to look more interesting. He could see something poking out of the envelope but couldn't make out the detail.

James looked around him as he closed in on the envelope like a buzzard stalking its prey. There was no one in view, so he clandestinely stopped and picked it up. He took a quick look inside the envelope, and all he could see was money!

He very quickly folded the envelope and looking around again to ensure he hadn't been observed by anyone he put it into his pocket and continued to walk.

As he walked, he reached for his cigarette packet from his inside jacket pocket and stopped for a second as he lit it. He pulled deeply on the cigarette and started to walk on towards the pub. Thinking about the envelope, his mind started racing wondering how much was in there. *This is wrong* was his first thought to himself. This could be some bloke's wages that he's taking home to his wife to pay the rent and look after the kids. He suddenly felt a pang of guilt momentarily surge through his body. However, the feeling was fleeting. James looked around him again to see if anyone was walking along, looking for something they may have lost, but there was no one in sight. He decided at this point that when he got to the pub, he would look to see if it contained an address or any other indication of who it may belong to and he promised himself he would work out how to return it to them. *You never know,* he thought, *there may be a reward.* He felt a lot better about it now.

He arrived at the pub and did the usual walk to the far end of the building to take up his favourite position at the bar. On the way, he passed all the usual faces standing in their desired position at the bar saying his hellos and shaking a few hands on the way. He always found it strange how people could become so territorial over a certain part of the bar in their local pub. He had seen it cause big arguments and even fights in the past. He had been using this pub for years.

It was a proper old-fashioned place with wooden floors and the walls painted in the colour of the local football team.

The regular customers ranged from barristers to the great unwashed, but everyone got on fine. It was a fine example of the melting pot that is London. There was the occasional bit of bother, but it was usually sorted out amongst the regulars. They had four large screen TVs on the walls to cover all kinds of sporting events, and at those times it could get very noisy and boisterous.

"Evening Jim," the barman called over to him whilst serving a pint of Guinness for an elderly gentleman sitting at the opposite end of the bar. "Usual?" he inquired.

"Please Will," James replied. He removed his wallet from the back pocket of his jeans and took out a crisp new £10 note. "Leave one in for Terry as well please," he added.

The barman placed a pint of lager in front of James and took the £10 note, after ringing the two drinks into the till he returned with some change and handed it to James. After about ten minutes of discussing the coming weekend's football and the like, James excused himself and went off to the toilets. As he entered a guy coming out smiled at him, "In one end and out the other, what a waste of money," he continued now roaring at laughter at his well-worn joke (which any man who has ever used a pub toilet will have heard a hundred times). James just smiled, nodded and continued on his way.

Once inside, he realised that he was alone. He went into one of the cubicles and locked the door. Reaching into his pocket, he pulled out the envelope which he had found earlier. He examined the front and back of the envelope looking for some clue as to who it belonged to, but there was nothing. He opened the envelope slowly and removed the contents. He quickly looked through for a payslip, business card or anything that may indicate where it came from but again nothing. He started to count the money. *Jesus!* he thought as he finished counting. Eight hundred and fifty quid. *Nearly two weeks of wages,* he thought to himself. He stared for what seemed an age at the money in his hand, wondering what he should do with it. There was no indication where it came from or whose it was. In one sense, this was a relief. It meant he could avoid the great moral dilemma as to what to do with it. He considered taking it to the police station, but you hear all these stories of things going missing when there's no ID. Unless someone comes in the pub asking about it in the next hour, I'm keeping it he quickly decided.

James put the money back into the envelope and returned into the bar to find his mate Terry already halfway through the pint that he had bought him.

"Where you been mate," Terry asked as James picked up his pint.

"Just having a piss," he replied.

Terry had been mates with James since they were kids. He was another of life's confirmed bachelors, his yearning for women was more in line with an overnight relationship rather than long term, and although he was not a particularly attractive man, his extreme confidence and smooth line in patter produced quite a decent strike rate when it came to the opposite sex. He had connections with some of the areas seedier faces and managed to get himself involved in some quite financially advantageous, though dubious, schemes. "What are we doing tonight then?" said Terry. "It's Friday. We gotta do something?"

"I'm not sure," James replied. "I may just stay here for a few. There's a band on later, might be a laugh."

"No," Terry said, sneering at the idea. "I've seen them before they're not all that. Let's go to a club we might meet a couple of sorts."

"I don't know mate," James said, looking very disinterested.

"If you're short of money, I can help you out?" offered Terry.

"Oh no, it's not that," smiled James thinking of the envelope sitting pretty in his pocket.

"Is that Lisa coming down here tonight?" asked Terry.

"Not sure," James replied.

"I bet she is," said Terry, "That's why you want to stay here isn't it in case she turns up? For fuck's sake, you need to either tell her how you feel or forget about it. You ain't gonna pull her by acting like her big brother."

Terry was the only person that James had talked about his feelings for Lisa, and he sometimes wished he hadn't. It was so difficult with them living together. If he told her how he felt and it freaked her out, she would be off, and then he'd never see her. He had decided to wait until the time was right, and it probably wasn't going to be in the near future. They had kissed a couple of times after a skin full of booze, but they had never gone any further, and even the kisses had never been spoken about again. *One day,* James thought to himself, *one day.*

Friday night football had just started on the TV when Lisa walked through the door. As usual, all the heads turned, and comments shouted at her were met with a perfect riposte every time.

Terry looked over at James with a big smile on his face. "Well, fancy that," he said, laughing. "Look who's turned up."

"Piss off, Terry," said Lisa.

"Pack it in you two," James interrupted. "Why can't you ever be civil to each other?" he asked.

"We are nice to each other. Just not when you're about, isn't that right darling?" said Terry laughing.

"I think Lisa was right the first time, piss off Terry," said James and he and Lisa both laughed.

"What you drinking then, Lisa?" Terry asked.

James looked up at the clock. He'd been in the pub over two hours, and no one had been in asking about the envelope. He'd been outside a few times for a smoke and saw no one wandering around looking for anything. *Sod it*, he thought. Putting his hand into the envelope in his pocket, he managed to peel a single top note out of his pocket.

"No, I'll get these," he said, producing a £50 note.

"Fuck me," said Terry, laughing. "You robbed a bank or something?"

"No, I had a bit of luck on the horses today," replied James "I didn't know you were a gambler James," Lisa said with a puzzled look on her face.

"It was just a one-off. A mate of mine had a tip for a horse, so we got on it. Came in at 20/1," he said.

"I'll have a large one then," said Terry.

James bought drinks for himself, Lisa, Terry, plus three other regulars at the bar.

"That's £22.50 please," the barman told James.

"Get the Guv'nor one and of course one for yourself," said James passing him the £50 note.

"Thank you very much," the barman replied.

It was a lovely feeling for James to be able to buy a big round at the bar. He didn't earn great money, and after paying his rent, for his car and various other payments he had, he couldn't afford to be generous in the pub too often. Terry, on the other hand, always seemed to have plenty of dough. James could never work out how. He didn't have a particularly well-paid job, but he had his own flat, drove a nice Mercedes and always seemed to have money. Still tonight James could hold his end up when it came to the drinks.

The evening continued to be enjoyable for James. Any feelings of guilt over the money seemed to recede with every pint. The band were pretty good, and when they played a couple of slow numbers, James even plucked up the courage to ask Lisa for a dance. Both times she agreed and holding her on the dance floor was like a dream to James. After a lot of alcohol had been consumed, most of it paid for by the by now extremely generous James, he suggested they all go to the local curry house.

"My treat," James shouted as they prepared to leave the pub.

Entering the restaurant was about the last memory he had when he awoke the next morning. The sun breaking through the partially closed curtains woke him. He was still fully dressed and lying on the couch in the living room. He could still taste the heady mix of beer, fags and curry. Lisa lay peacefully sleeping next to him (also fully clothed) with her arm across his chest. As he tried to move, Lisa stirred and slowly opening her eyes, she smiled at James. "Don't go," she said now wrapping her other arm around him.

Wow, thought James, *What on earth happened last night?*

"Do you want coffee?" he asked her.

"Please," she replied in a very sleepy voice.

James pulled himself away from her and made his way to the kitchen. As he prepared the cups and boiled the kettle, James racked his brains to try and remember what had happened the night before and how he and Lisa had ended up entwined on the sofa.

As the kettle came to the boil, he lifted it and poured the steaming water into the cups. After adding milk and sugar, he stirred them both and carried them back into the living room. Lisa was now sitting up on the sofa with her legs tucked up neatly beneath her, and even at this time of the morning, she looked beautiful to him.

"That was a good night," James said, kind of hoping that Lisa would give him some clue as to how it ended.

"It was lovely, James. I've never seen you so full of confidence and bubbly," Lisa said. "But then I've never seen you so generous before either," she laughed.

"Do you mind if I ask how we ended up sleeping together on the sofa?" James enquired.

"You don't remember?" Lisa asked with a mischievous grin on her face. "Spending all that money can turn a girl's head, you know," she continued, again laughing.

"What?" inquired James.

"You were spending like it was going out of fashion last night. Perhaps you should bet on the horses more often," she said.

"What horses?" James asked.

"The horse that came in at 20/1," she replied.

Suddenly the memories came flooding back. The envelope with all the money. Shit, what had he done?

"Oh. That horse," he said.

"No, I think that was a one-off."

"What a shame," Lisa said. "I could get used to being treated like that." She again gave James that mischievous smile.

"I am more concerned about what happened when we got home," said James.

"You were a perfect gentleman," Lisa assured him. "We just had a few more dances and collapsed onto the sofa. You were sleeping within seconds. I felt so comfortable there with you. I decided to stay. Is that OK?" she asked.

"Of course, any time," he said.

James finished his coffee and went into his bedroom. Feeling in his pockets, there was no sign of the envelope. He looked around the room and couldn't see it anywhere. His heart started racing. He casually re-entered the living room and looked around, still no sign of it.

"Are you looking for this?" Lisa asked, holding up the opened envelope.

"Yes, where was it?" he inquired.

"You put it under the sofa last night. You kept saying no one should know you had it," she said.

As she passed it over to him, a piece of pink-coloured paper fell out of the envelope and onto the sofa.

"You really had the gambling bug yesterday, you bought two lines on the lottery as well," she said as she passed the ticket to him.

"Oh yeah, I'd forgotten about that," he lied.

James walked back into his room and looked at the lottery ticket for the previous evening's Euro-millions. He hadn't noticed the ticket in the envelope when he first looked through, but then he was more interested in the hard cash. He lay on his bed and thought about the money, the guilt building up inside him again, *I'm going to find out who's it was,* he thought to himself, *I only have to put back what I spent last night, and everything will be fine.* He counted what money was left. He sat on the edge of his bed with a bewildered look on his face.

How the fuck had he spent £470 in one night? We'll that ruined that plan. He couldn't possibly put that much money back in. He would have to just keep quiet about it and stick to the horse story.

Lisa had turned the TV on, and James could vaguely hear a news report about a tragedy that had occurred somewhere overnight. As he lay there feeling guilty about the money, Lisa came running into his room.

"Where's your lottery ticket?" she asked. "There's only one winner, and they are English," she said excitedly.

James slowly took the pink piece of paper from his pocket and handed it to Lisa, who ran back into the living room and dropped onto the sofa.

After a minute or so, James looked up to see Lisa standing in the doorway of his bedroom, looking shocked and slightly pale. "You've bleedin', got it," she said in a very calm voice.

"Got what?" asked James, dreading to hear what she was about to say.

"You've got the bloody winning Lottery numbers," she said very quietly. "All of them," her voice quivering with disbelief.

James leapt from his bed and took the ticket from Lisa. He rushed into the living room and looked at the screen. Lisa had logged in via the red button, and the numbers were on the screen:

6 14 21 32 46 – Lucky Stars 8 & 11

He read the numbers and checked them with his ticket. Suddenly the guilt he felt over an envelope that contained £850 had increased by £72 million!!!

"Oh my God!" said Lisa, still looking stunned. "You have to phone them, I think."

"I need a lie down first," said James as he walked into his room and collapsed on his bed.

Within seconds Lisa came in, "Can I join you?" she asked.

Without looking at her, James just nodded.

They lay there neither talking, both a bit shell shocked by the events of the morning.

Chapter 3

Joan Maclaren was sitting having her mid-day cup of tea and biscuit. Her mind was full of past memories. She enjoyed this time of day. She would often sit and talk to the picture of her departed husband, Jack, which sat upon the TV. She was only 72 but had been a widow now for 28 years after her husband had been shot dead by a local gang when he was just 46. As she always explained to people, "My Jack was no angel, but he didn't deserve what he got." She had then been responsible for raising her three sons aged 11, 14 and 16. They had been in trouble most of their lives, but to her, they were angels, and they were always there to look after their dear mum. She was just finishing her tea when she heard a key turning in her front door.

"Hello, Mum. It's only me," called her youngest son, Billy. Billy Maclaren was known locally as one not to be messed with, and although he was the youngest brother, he was the one with the brains, and for this reason, he ran the family business. The business consisted of three scrap yards and a couple of car showrooms and as far as Mum was concerned that was it. There were, however, other business deals going down that Mum would never be aware of.

"Hello, Billy," she called to him as he came down the hallway.

"Cup of tea, Luv?" she asked.

"No time, Mum. Just a fleeting visit," he replied.

Billy entered the living room and promptly helped himself to a couple of biscuits.

"Mum I need a favour," Billy said. "I've got some money here, and I need it deposited into the bank."

"OK Love. I've got to go to the shop later. I can do it then."

"Thanks, Mum. You are an angel," he replied. "There's £800 in this envelope and here's the paying-in book," he said as he handed her the envelope.

Joan took the money from the envelope and started counting it. When she had finished, she started counting it again.

"What's the problem?" Billy asked.

"Well, I make it £850 here," she replied.

Billy's face lit up with a big smile as he looked at his Mum and said, "That must be your bit for going."

Joan slapped her baby boy, playfully on the knee and smiled at him.

"You boys spoil me," she said, returning his smile.

"OK Mum, you be careful carrying that money around with you. I'll be over tomorrow to see you." Although it was a lot of money for an old lady to be carrying around, he knew that she was a tough old girl and everyone in the manor knew who she was. More importantly, everyone knew who her sons were. *She'll be OK,* he thought.

Billy left and went about his business while Mum started preparing her lunch.

Joan ate her lunch of liver, bacon, peas and gravy and had a little nap in the armchair only to be woken by the incessant cheering and clapping which accompanied all mundane daytime quiz shows. She turned off the TV and realising it was already 3:00 pm set about getting herself ready to go out.

After showering and dressing Joan left her first-floor flat and made her way along the corridor. She had lived here for 25 of the 28 years that she had been a widow. Her boys had continuously asked her to move out and offered to buy her a nice bungalow by the coast, but this was where her heart was, and she would never move away. She descended the stairs to the ground floor, where she saw Mrs Davies standing in her doorway.

"Good afternoon," Mrs Davies said, seeing Joan walking towards her.

"Hello, Luv," Joan replied.

"I'm off to the shops and the bank. Is there anything you need?" she asked.

"No, I'm fine thanks, my Jane came round earlier with my shopping," Mrs Davies answered.

Jane was her daughter and did most of her shopping as she couldn't move about too well, but Joan always stopped just in case she needed anything.

Joan bade Mrs Davies farewell and set off for the bus stop. She only waited for about five minutes, and her bus arrived. She boarded and took a seat for the five-minute journey to the high street. Once off the bus, Joan went first to the supermarket where she picked up a few bits including some lovely looking pork chops for her Sunday lunch. Once everything was loaded into her pull along trolley, she made her way to the bank. On her arrival, she couldn't believe her eyes. The queue for the bank came out of the door and down past the butchers next door. She checked her watch and saw that it was nearly 4:00 pm. The bank closed in half an hour, and it looked unlikely that the queue would be gone by then. *I'll leave the bank until the morning,* Joan thought to herself.

She continued to walk along the High Street to her next port of call, the newsagent.

"Good afternoon, Mrs Maclaren," the man behind the counter called to her as she entered the shop. "How are you?" he added.

"I'm fine thanks," she answered, stopping at the Lottery display and taking a pen from the dispenser. She put her bag down and started to fill out her EuroMillions lottery ticket due to be drawn that evening. She had been using the same numbers for about five years. They were a combination of people's birthdays, ages and anniversaries, and she knew both lines off by heart.

She took the slip to the checkout and handed it over to the shop keeper.

"Let's hope these are lucky for you this week," he said with a smile.

"I don't know why I bother," said Joan, laughing, "I never win a penny!"

She opened her bag and put the lottery ticket in the envelope with the money.

Joan looked back towards the bank as she left the shop, but the queue was still just as long. She turned the other way and decided to go and visit her lifelong friend Dawn, who lived just around the corner.

As she reached Dawn's house, she saw her friend coming out of the door and walking towards a minicab parked outside.

"Dawn!" she called out.

Her friend saw her coming and gestured for the cab to wait. "Hello, Joan," she said. "I'm just off down to the hospital to see my sister. Do you want to come?"

"No," replied Joan.

"I've got all this shopping with me. I don't fancy dragging it all the way down the hospital," she said. "I only popped round to see if you fancied coming over for a bit of lunch on Sunday. I've just bought some lovely pork chops."

"I'll take you up on that," said Dawn.

"What time?" she inquired.

"About one OK for you?" June asked.

"Sounds great," replied Dawn, "See you on Sunday."

"Bye." they both called out at the same time.

As Dawn's cab pulled away, Joan turned to walk back towards the high street. She walked along the quiet side street towards the bustle of the high street, and she reflected on how different the whole area had been in her younger days. As she did, she was suddenly aware of someone coming up quickly behind her. She turned to see who it was, and two young lads came speeding past her on their pushbikes, almost knocking her over. She lost her grip on the trolley, and it fell to the ground spilling the contents of her handbag onto the pavement. Joan turned towards the two youths cycling away and laughing. "Bloody yobs!" she shouted, but they were long gone.

Jean bent down to pick up her trolley, feeling a little shocked and started to walk slowly along the road. As she got to the corner, she stopped outside the pub and had a quick look through the window. She could almost see her Jack sitting at the bar with their three little boys running around him. She shook her head and felt a tear come to her eye. With a deep breath, she continued her walk back to the bus stop.

A bus journey and a short walk later Joan was back indoors with the kettle and her slippers on ready for a lazy night in front of her favourite soap operas.

At about 9:00 pm, she made herself another cup of tea and was off to bed to read her book and get a good night's sleep. As she felt her eyes closing her last thought was, *I must get down to the bank for Billy in the morning.*

Joan woke early on Saturday morning and went straight to the kitchen and filled the kettle. She made her cup of tea and walked slowly into the living room. She sat in her favourite armchair and placed her tea on the small occasional table that sat directly beside her. She picked up the TV remote and pressed the buttons to find BBC News. An awful tragedy had occurred overnight in the Middle East, and the programme was going back and forth from the studio to the scene of the tragedy. After a few minutes of this, Joan was getting bored. The next story on the news was that someone from the UK had won last night's Euro Millions worth £72 million. She picked up the remote control again and pressed the red button. She then navigated herself to the lottery results.

6 14 21 32 46 Lucky Stars 8 & 11

She sat looking aghast for a moment. "Those are my numbers!" she said out loud.

"No, they really are," she said as if arguing with herself.

She sat in her chair, stunned just staring at the screen convinced she had won but frightened to look away in case they changed. Getting up very slowly, Joan moved over to her handbag and bought it back to her armchair. She sat and unzipped the bag, and frantically started searching for the envelope containing both Billy's money and her Lottery ticket. *It's not here*, she thought, suddenly starting to panic. She turned her bag upside down and let all the contents fall to the floor. As she looked down, she could see her purse, her bus pass, her keys and various other bits and pieces but no envelope.

She went to her coat and searched through the pockets, but it was not there.

Joan could feel tears starting to well up in her eyes. Strangely the tears were not for the £72 million but for the money of Billy's that she had lost. He had entrusted her with his money, and she had lost it.

Joan spent the next two hours searching her little flat for the envelope. Going over every inch of the apartment again and again in the hope that she may find it. It wasn't there.

Chapter 4

James had been lying on his bed with the delightful Lisa sleeping next to him for the last hour. He turned on his side and looked at her, and for a moment, he was lost in her beauty. At that moment, he came back to reality. He was probably at the biggest turning point in his life. His quest for Lisa seemed to be gaining momentum, and he had riches beyond belief, but for all that, he knew it was wrong.

Lisa stirred and opened her eyes, she blinked and focused and realised she was looking directly into James eyes.

"Hello, my millionaire friend," she said with a smile. "Have you phoned the Lottery people yet?" she asked.

"No, not yet," James replied. "I think I'm going to leave it a couple of days and let the dust settle. In the meantime, I would appreciate it if you keep this just between the two of us," he said.

"Whatever you want, are you not going to tell Terry?" she inquired.

"God, no," replied James. "He's the last person I want knowing about this at the moment."

"Anyway, I'm starving. Fancy an early lunch?" James asked.

James rose from the bed and went into the kitchen. After going through the cupboards and the fridge, he could find nothing that took his fancy.

"Get yourself ready we'll go out for lunch," he said.

"Do you think you can afford it?" Lisa asked with a smile.

"Just get ready," James replied.

Thirty minutes later, James and Lisa left the house and headed towards the train station.

"Where are we going?" asked Lisa.

"I don't know," replied James, "I thought we could go into town and find somewhere a bit better than the greasy spoon on the high street."

"You're spoiling me again," Lisa said as she slipped her arm through his.

They bought their tickets and waited for about five minutes on the platform until the train arrived. They boarded the train to Victoria and fourteen minutes later were alighting in the heart of London. London is a magnificent city, and Lisa liked nothing better than wandering the streets, observing people going about their business and taking in the sights. The architecture was fantastic, and the history behind many of the buildings made her very proud to be a Londoner. Being in the heart of London always reminded her of her mother. They would pack sandwiches and drinks and head off into town during the school holidays and spend hours in Hyde Park sitting by the Serpentine watching people swimming, and sun-bathing whilst she and Mum would eat their picnic.

"I do love London in the autumn," Lisa said. "Not so many tourists around. It gives us a chance to really appreciate our wonderful city."

"Do you like London?" she asked.

"It's just nice to be away from the same old area and the same old people," he replied.

"I imagine you'll be spending a lot of time in swanky places from now on James?" she said.

"Really?" said James. "Do you really see me as a flashy sort of person?" he asked.

"Well no, but with all the money you have now you won't want to be spending time in The Crown with the likes of me, will you?"

"I may slum it now and again," James replied, laughing.

"At last," said Lisa.

"At last what?" asked James.

"That's the first time you've smiled since you found out you won all that money," she said.

"Well, they do say it doesn't bring you happiness," retorted James.

"I know," said Lisa, "but I didn't think you became unhappy instantly."

James laughed, and as he turned to look at Lisa, he had an incredible urge to kiss her, which he resisted as he had so many times before.

"I think I'm probably in shock," he said.

"So where are we eating?" Lisa asked.

"Anywhere you want my dear," James replied.

"OK, close your eyes and give me your hand," she said.

James did as he was told and let Lisa guide him along the road. After about fifteen paces, they went through a doorway, and once inside, Lisa said, "OK, you can open your eyes now."

James opened his eyes to find himself standing in McDonald's.

"Is this it?" he said, "We're in Central London with a choice of all these fantastic restaurants, and you choose McDonald's?"

"Well, I don't want you to think I only want you for your money," she said with a smile. "Besides, I wanted to know that wherever we went I was with the richest man in the place and you're never sure around here."

"OK, what will it be then?" he asked.

"Can I have a Happy Meal?" Lisa said.

"Only if we get to share the toy," James quipped.

They went to the counter and as promised James bought Lisa a Happy Meal and got himself a Big Mac and fries. They saw a booth at the back of the restaurant, and Lisa shot over there to claim it.

James followed carrying a tray full of food and smiling.

"Hey, you're smiling again," said Lisa.

"It's not easy to be unhappy around you," James replied. They sat down and began to unwrap their food. Lisa was delighted with the toy which came with her meal although she had to rely on James to put it together for her.

After they had finished eating and were drinking coffee, Lisa looked at James and asked, "So what are you going to do with all this money?"

"I have absolutely no idea at the moment," he replied.

"You must have thought about it in the past?" she said. "Everyone has had that conversation about what they would do if they won the lottery."

"Not me," said James, "I never do the lottery."

"Never?" she said.

"No, never," he reiterated.

They both went very quiet for a moment lost in their own thoughts. James was wondering whether he should tell her the truth but wasn't sure, Lisa had something else on her mind.

"You say you never do the lottery?" Lisa asked.

"That's right," said James.

"And you never bet on horses?" she continued.

"That's correct," James replied.

"But yesterday you won shit loads of money on a horse, and then you won the lottery," she said.

"Mmm, very true," said James. Wondering where this was going.

"Well, that's amazing. I think you should go to press and tell your story. They would probably make a film about you." With that, she started laughing.

"I will certainly not be asking for any publicity," he said. "I've told you this is our secret."

"I know," said Lisa. "I was only playing, don't be so serious." They drained their coffee cups and, rising from the table, put all their wrappers on the tray and emptied it into the rubbish chute.

Once outside, Lisa took James arm again, and they started to walk along Regent Street. Lisa insisted on a look around 'Hamleys' toy store where James bought her a small teddy bear.

"What are you going to call him?" James asked.

"I don't know," she replied. "What about Lotto?" she suggested.

"I'm not sure about that," James said.

"I know, I'll name it after the horse that you won on yesterday," she suggested. "What was it called?"

"Err, I don't remember," he said with a slight stammer.

"You don't remember?" she said rather puzzled. "You won all that money on a horse, and you don't remember what it was called?"

"I didn't put the bet on," he replied, "It was the guy at work. I just gave him the money."

"Who?" she asked.

"Who, what?" he said, trying to buy himself a bit of thinking time.

"Who was the guy who put the bet on?" she asked.

"I'm not sure. He was a temp," he replied.

"So, some bloke who you don't know gives you a tip for an unnamed horse, and you just give him money to go and place a bet for you?" she said.

"Pretty much so," he replied.

"I'm surprised he came back at all really," she said, shaking her head. "I can see I'm going to have to look after you when you get all this money, or you'll be giving it away to every Tom, Dick or Harry who comes along," she smiled reassuringly at him.

James mind was racing. He was so torn as to what he should do. He so wanted to tell Lisa, but that would just put pressure on her. His mind went back to the envelope, and whoever had dropped it. All of this should have been theirs not his, but could he give up this opportunity now it had been dropped into his lap? One thing was certain, he needed a drink. Keeping this secret was gnawing away at him.

Chapter 5

Billy Maclaren hated having to work on a Saturday morning, but he had a special delivery coming today. He stood in the port-a-cabin which was used as his office looking out of the window. This was one of three scrap yards that the family owned and was nicely tucked away in a dead-end road in the back streets of South London. A perfect location for some of the shadier deals he carried out. This yard had a special place in his heart. This was his dad's first yard. Originally it belonged to a guy called Joey Richards, but legend has it that Jack Maclaren Sr. had won it in a game of cards, however other stories indicated that Joey didn't have much choice once Jack had decided it was going to be his yard.

Billy looked across the three huge piles of smashed vehicles piled one on top of the other. It took him back to his childhood when he and his brothers would spend hours climbing over the wreckage playing all manner of games before his dad would come out and shout at them.

He heard laughter from outside, rose from his chair and walked around his desk to the window of the portacabin. He looked out into the scrap yard and saw two young lads that were chatting and smoking. Opening the window, he shouted.

"Oi, get those fucking cars moved. I've got a lorry on the way with four more scrappers coming in about half an hour. Now get a fucking move on or get another job."

The two young guys immediately dropped their cigarettes and stamped them out. One mounted the forklift truck, and the other went straight over to the vehicles that needed moving.

"Pair of wankers," Billy said to his brother Jack.

Jack was the eldest of the brothers and named quite aptly after his father to whom he bore an amazing resemblance. Jack had never been overly endowed in the brain capacity, but when it came to the heavy side of the work, there were very few who could touch him. He was a true grafter. Standing 6ft 3in tall and weighing about nineteen stone he was a huge man, extremely handy with his fists but was just as happy with a baseball bat or gun. Three times Jack had been arrested and charged with murder, and every time he had got away with it. The police had suspected jury tampering or witness intimidation in each case but had never been able to pin it on him. He was quite simply one of South London's hardest criminals. Years before, when the area was controlled by another family, Jack and his brother Peter – with the help of some willing friends – decided to close down their business. For about six months, shops and businesses were firebombed, members of the other gang were found beaten senseless, and those who weren't had the good sense to go into hiding. When the dust settled the dethroned family could be found in such places as Spain and Cyprus. This area of South London now belonged to the Maclaren's.

"Where the fuck do you get these staff from?" said Jack. "One of them is Bobby Collins' son, I promised him I'd look after the boy," said Billy.

"Bobby's a knob," said Jack.

"I know," said Billy. "But he's useful to have on our side."

"I suppose you're right," said Jack. "But I think…"

"Well don't think," said Billy interrupting his elder brother. "I do the thinking, OK?" Jack started to laugh.

"You little shit," he said. "I think you spent too much time at school." Again, Jack laughed out loud.

Billy went over to the window again and saw the two young lads moving the second of the cars with the forklift.

"Almost done," he said, more to himself than to his brother.

Billy looked at his watch.

"They should be here in about ten minutes, Jack. Get the bag out of the safe and wait here until I call you, then bring it down. OK?" said Billy.

"Got it," Jack replied.

"Are you tooled up?" Billy asked.

"Of course," said Jack. "Wouldn't go anywhere without it." An evil smile came across Jack's face as he produced a 38mm Glock handgun.

"OK, keep it well hidden. There shouldn't be any problems but just in case," said Billy.

Five minutes later, there was a knock on the door, and one of the young lads entered.

"There's a lorry pulling up outside Mr Maclaren," he said.

"Thanks, son," he replied.

Billy looked over to the window, and he could see the flatbed lorry with four well smashed up cars loaded up pulling into the yard.

He made his way down the stairs and over to the lorry. The driver was just jumping down from his cab as Billy got to it. "Hello Kenny," Billy said, extending his right hand towards the slightly overweight and very dirty looking man.

"Alright, Bill," he replied, shaking Billy's outstretched hand.

"You on your own?" he asked.

Billy laughed.

"You know me better than that," said Billy. "Jack's upstairs, he'll be down in a moment." Kenny's face changed expression.

"Oh good, it'll be nice to see him," he said unconvincingly.

"By the way, Kenny, your three blokes have been sitting in a car over the road for about twenty minutes. I suggest you tell them to fuck off because you wouldn't want Jack to get the idea you don't trust us would you," Billy said in a whisper.

Kenny looked embarrassed. "It wasn't my idea Billy, Honest," he said.

"Just get them the fuck away from my yard before I tell Jack they're here," Billy said in a menacing tone.

Kenny retrieved his mobile phone from the cab, and after a matter of seconds, Billy saw the car drive away with all three men still inside.

Billy called the two young lads over and instructed them to remove three of the vehicles and stack them on the pile and move the fourth one into the workshop.

Whilst Billy and Kenny had a chat catching up on bits of gossip from the criminal world, the two young operatives set about their task. Fifteen minutes later all the cars were in their place, and Billy had told the two youngsters they could go. He arranged to meet them later in the pub for their wages.

"Jack!" Billy called.

The door to the office opened, and Jack came down the stairs carrying a large holdall. Kenny looked visibly nervous. Being on his own with Billy and Jack Maclaren was not something he would like to make a habit of.

"Right, come on then," Billy said, walking over to the workshop. "Let's get this done."

Jack and Kenny followed him, and all three entered the workshop to find a rusting Ford Mondeo sitting there.

"You got the keys, Kenny," Billy asked.

Kenny produced the keys and handed them to Billy who opened the boot. Inside was a briefcase which Billy removed and placed on the workbench.

"Kenny, open it please," said Billy.

"Where's the money?" Kenny asked. His question was met by a look from Jack that almost froze him to the spot. "You'll get your fucking money. Now just open it." Billy was getting agitated now.

Kenny did as he was told and opened the case. The case contained four bags of white powder. Billy took a knife from his jacket pocket and flicked it open. He put the knife through the plastic outer of one of the bags and pulled it out with some of the white powder still on the blade. He put some of the powder on to his finger and then rubbed it onto his gums. He waited for a moment as Kenny looked on nervously.

"That's fine," Billy eventually said, much to Kenny's relief.

"Give him the holdall Jack."

Jack passed the holdall to Kenny, and he opened it and had a quick look inside. He didn't bother counting the money, he just wanted to get out of there.

"Thanks, Kenny, nice doing business with you," said Billy.

"Likewise," said Kenny as he started to leave.

As Kenny walked to his lorry, Billy turned to Jack and said, "He had three blokes waiting over the road. I think perhaps he didn't trust us, Jack."

"Oh, did he?" Jack replied.

As Kenny was about to ascend to the cab of his lorry, he suddenly felt the full force of a baseball bat make contact with the rear of his head. He fell back to the floor and looked up to see Jack bearing down on him with the bloodied baseball bat. Jack hit him twice in each leg before Billy gave him the signal to back off.

Billy walked over to where Kenny lay in a bloody heap on the floor and leant over him.

"Now, let me tell you something, Kenny. I like you, but I will not have anyone implying that me or my brothers cannot be trusted in a business deal. Do you get that?" Billy said.

Kenny meekly nodded his head.

"On the other hand, my brother thinks you're a cunt and would happily kill you. So, I suggest you crawl over to the gates and wait outside for your shit mates to come and collect you. We need to go, and we will be locking the yard now. You will be able to pick your lorry up on Monday morning. Now get yourself moving, or I will have to lock you in here with the dogs. Fucking move!"

Kenny scurried across the ground, praying he would escape the yard without any further punishment. Billy went back into the workshop and took the briefcase. He climbed the stairs to the office and put the case straight into the safe.

As he came down the stairs, he saw Kenny sitting on the pavement outside with his back against the wall. As he got to the bottom of the stairs, he called to his brother, "Let the dogs free Jack."

Jack made his way over to the kennels to release two lean and menacing Dobermans. Orbit and Spike started jumping around and barking as Jack came towards them. He unlocked the gate and entered the pen. Both dogs jumped up at him and licked him profusely as Jack just stood there and laughed. He unchained the dogs and let them free.

Billy walked past Kenny's lorry and picked up the holdall that Jack had given him earlier. He walked through the gate, and Jack pulled it closed behind him and started to lock up.

"Don't forget your money Kenny," Billy said, throwing the bag at him. "As I said, we can always be trusted, but you just had to learn the hard way didn't you."

Billy and Jack walked over to Billy's car and got in.

"Fancy a pint and a sandwich?" Billy asked.

"Sounds good to me," Jack replied.

"OK, just need to pop in and see Mum on the way," said Billy. The pair travelled the three miles through the Saturday lunchtime traffic to their Mum's flat. Billy parked up, and they both got out of the vehicle, he took his keys from his pocket as he walked up the stairs, inserted the keys and opened the front door.

"Hi Mum, it's Billy," he said as he walked towards the lounge. "I've got Jack with me."

"Is the kettle on Mum?" Jack called out. There was no response.

They entered the living room and saw Mum sitting in her armchair, still wearing her nightclothes and holding the photo of her beloved husband. As they moved closer, she looked up at them, and they could see she had been crying.

"What's up, Mum?" Jack asked.

"Something terrible has happened," she said, her eyes filling with tears as she looked at her two boys.

"What's happened?" Billy asked.

"I've lost your money, Billy," she said.

Jack gave Billy an enquiring look.

"I asked Mum to put some money in the bank for me," Billy said.

"How much?" Jack asked.

"Eight hundred quid," he replied.

"You let Mum walk around with that sort of money on her?" Jack said, giving Billy a look of disgust.

"Jack, leave it," said their mum.

"What happened then?" asked Billy.

Joan told the boys of her journey to the bank and that she couldn't get in because of the queue. She told them that she had gone to see Dawn and then came home.

"Did anybody stop you or talk to you at all?" asked Billy. "Two boys rode past me on their pushbikes as I was walking down Church Street and nearly knocked me down, but they didn't stop me," she told them.

"And you didn't go anywhere else?" Billy asked.

"Only into the newsagent for my lottery ticket," she said. As she did, her eyes started to well up with tears again.

"Mum, it's only £850, don't worry about it," Jack said.

"But I put my lottery ticket in the envelope as well," she said. "I shouldn't worry about that, you never win anyway," Billy said, laughing and trying to lighten the mood.

"That's the thing," she said, "I did win!"

"What!" exclaimed Billy.

"Well, I always do the same numbers. They're all birthdays and anniversaries. I know them all off by heart, and this morning I looked them up, and I had won. I'm not talking a tenner – the big one," she said.

The two brothers looked at each other in amazement.

"Are you sure?" asked Jack.

"Yes, look I'll show you," she said, pressing the red button on the remote control, she navigated to the lottery results. The boys sat there as she got a sheet of paper from the drawer. On the paper were two lists of numbers the second list corresponded exactly with the numbers on the TV.

"How much have you won?" Billy asked.

"£72 million, give or take," Joan said, starting to get tearful again.

Jack and Billy stared at each other in disbelief.

"OK, let's go over this again," said Billy. "After you went to the newsagents you went to Dawn's house and then walked down Church Street, got the bus and came home. Is that right?"

"Yes," said Joan.

"Did anyone sit next to you on the bus?" asked Jack.

"No, Mrs Baker's boy Darren was driving the bus, so I sat at the front talking to him. There were only about three other people on the bus," she added.

"So, the nearest you came into contact with anybody was the two yobbos on their bikes in Church Street. Correct?" asked Billy.

"Yes," she replied.

"Is there any chance you could have dropped the envelope when they came by you?" asked Jack.

"Well, my trolley fell over, and I had to bend down to pick it up. I suppose it could have fallen out," Joan said.

"OK Mum, we are going to go and see if it's lying around anywhere and put the word about to see if anyone picked it up," Billy said. "I'll call you later with any news."

"Thank you, boys, I'm so sorry about your money Billy," Joan said tearfully.

"Forget about it, Mum," he said and gave her a big reassuring smile.

Billy and Jack both kissed her and left. They descended the stairs and walked to the car without saying a word.

"£72 million fucking quid," Jack said as Billy turned the ignition key.

"We've got to find that ticket," Billy said, "we'll start in Church Street, you never know."

They pulled into Church Street and got out of the car. Starting at the top of the road, they worked their way down to The Crown pub at the bottom of the road and saw nothing. "Fuck it," said Billy, "Let's go in the pub and see if anyone in there saw anything."

As they walked into the pub, a few heads turned and looked away very quickly.

"Hello, Billy, Jack," the landlord said as they walked in. "Long time no see," he added nervously. "What can I get you?"

"Hi Geoff, two pints of Carling please and five minutes of your time," Billy replied.

The landlord put the two pints on the bar.

"On the house," he said with a smile, "I'll be back in a couple of minutes."

"That's very kind," said Jack.

Billy was looking around the pub catching the eye of a few faces he knew and acknowledging them with a nod. The door opened, and a couple in their mid-twenties came in laughing as they walked to the far end of the bar.

"She's a bit tasty," Jack said, and the way Billy was looking at her showed he agreed.

Chapter 6

James and Lisa had to run across the concourse of Victoria Station to get to the platform in time to get their train back to the suburbs of South London. They jumped onto the train as the doors closed behind them and they started to move away.

"Wow only just made it," said Lisa, as they fell into their seats laughing.

"All that for a McDonald's lunch and a small teddy bear," laughed James.

"But it was fun, and it's a lovely teddy bear," replied Lisa hugging the still un-named bear.

"When we get back, I'm going to the Crown for a pint before I go home," said James. "Fancy it?" he asked her. "Why not, I could do with a livener," she replied.

The train journey once again lasted just fourteen minutes, and as they started to pull into their station, James rose from his seat.

"Come on," he said, "this is us."

Lisa rose from her seat and followed James off the train. As they came out of the station, Lisa linked her arm through James for the short walk to the pub.

When they entered the Crown, James noticed a couple of very dubious-looking characters sitting at the end of the bar. He had a feeling he'd seen them before but couldn't think where. As he looked towards the other end of the bar, he saw his mate Terry leaning on the bar and chatting to the barmaid. As they got to where Terry was standing, he paused his conversation with the barmaid and greeted them.

"Hiya mate," he said to James, "see you've got little Miss Snooty with you again."

"Yes, you best get used to it," Lisa replied much to James amazement.

"Just get the beers in Terry," James said to hide the fact that he was blushing a little after Lisa's comment.

Terry ordered the beers and turning to James, he whispered. "See those two blokes at the end of the bar?"

"Yes," replied James.

"Two of the Maclaren brothers. Jack and Billy, the other one, Pete, has just finished doing a bit of bird," he said.

"Shit, I've heard of them," said James. "What are they doing in here?"

"Not sure but for all our sakes let's hope it's a friendly visit," warned Terry.

Their drinks arrived, and James passed Lisa's half of cider to her.

"Those blokes at the other end of the bar keep looking at me," she said to James indicating she meant the Maclaren brothers.

"Just ignore them, Lisa, they're dangerous," James explained. The three of them moved to the corner at the end of the bar and stood in a position where Lisa wasn't visible to the Maclaren's. She felt much more comfortable.

"Good night last night, mate," Terry said to James. "Nice to see you shelling out for a change."

"Very funny," James replied. "Do you know how much I spent?"

"No, go on, surprise me," Terry said.

"Over four hundred quid," James replied.

"Well if you will offer to take half the pub to the curry house what do you expect?" Terry told him. "You probably won't be able to afford to come out for another month," he laughed. Lisa just smiled and looked at James, who lowered his head and tried not to grin.

"Be back in a moment," Lisa said as she went in search of the Ladies.

"Well?" Terry asked.

"Well, what?" James looked at Terry puzzled.

"You and Lisa, did you?" Terry winked at James.

"No, we didn't. We're just mates," James replied.

"I saw you walk over from the station arm-in-arm," Terry said.

"Let's just say things are moving in the right direction," James smiled.

"I bet it is," Terry said, laughing. "I'm just going for a smoke," he said as he started walking away.

As Terry got to the other end of the bar, James saw one of the Maclaren brothers stop him with a smile and a handshake. They continued chatting for a few minutes, and then Terry disappeared out of the door for his smoke. *That's strange*, thought James.

Lisa came back to the bar and finished her drink.

"I'm going home now, are you coming?" she asked James.

"No, I'm going to stay and have a couple more with Terry," he said. "Not sure what I'm doing later."

"OK, maybe see you later," she said, and with that, she leaned forward to give James a kiss. James, as usual, moved his face to one side in anticipation of a peck on the cheek.

"Really?" she said, placing her hands on either side of his face, she kissed him full on the lips. James felt his heart skip.

With that, she winked at him, turned on her heels and walked away. James, along with almost every other bloke in the pub, followed her with his eyes as she left.

Terry, who had been chatting with a guy further up the bar, re-joined James.

"Go on, Jimmy, my son," he said. "I saw that kiss, see what can happen when you open your wallet now and again," he laughed.

"I just saw you talking to one of those Maclaren brothers, how do you know them?" James asked.

"Our paths have crossed a few times," Terry replied.

"How?" inquired James.

"Just some little bits of business, that's all," said Terry.

"How on earth have your paths crossed in your line of business?" asked James.

"This and that, you know what I mean?" Terry said.

"Not really," said James. "He's a big-time villain, and you're a logistics manager for a funeral director. I hardly see where those two paths cross."

"Villains have to die too," said Terry with an impish grin on his face. "Fancy another pint?"

"Yeah, go on then," James replied, feeling somewhat uneasy about Terry's relationship with the underworld.

The Maclaren brothers had gone, and the whole atmosphere of the pub seemed to have lifted a couple of notches. Someone had put some sloshy romantic music on the jukebox, and James found himself staring into the distance with a smile on his face.

The two of them continued drinking and chatting and were joined by another mate Gary. The talk was mainly of football, women and all the other rubbish men talk about in a bar. Occasional banter with the bar staff or other customers ensued.

"What are we doing tonight then lads?" Terry asked.

"I'm up for a night out," Gary said.

At just that moment, James felt a vibration in his pocket. Taking out his phone, he saw he had a text message:

FANCY LASAGNE TONIGHT?
I'M COOKING. LISA XXX

James looked up from his phone, worried that he might be blushing, he was certainly smiling.

"Don't think I can make it tonight guys," he said and franticly started texting.

SOUNDS GREAT

James stared at his phone, awaiting a response. He didn't have to wait long.

OK BE HOME FOR 8:30 I'LL
HAVE EVERYTHING READY. XXX

James smiled and put his phone back into his pocket. He looked up at the clock above the bar it was 7:15 pm.

"Drink anyone?" James asked.

"Bloody hell!" said Gary, "Is this really you, James?" He and Terry both laughed, but at the same time, Terry had a strange look on his face.

"I told you, Gary, he's a new man," Terry said. "I think that Lisa has taken the padlock off his wallet!"

James watched the clock as it slowly moved round to 8:15 pm. Picking up his pint and draining the remains, he said his farewells and left. He walked up to the high street and into the off-licence for a bottle of chilled wine, and at precisely 8:27 pm, he put the key in the front door and opened it.

As he approached the open door of the lounge, he noticed that the table had been moved into the centre of the room and laid with cutlery and napkins.

He went into the kitchen, and Lisa was standing at the oven wearing oven gloves ready to remove the steaming hot lasagne from the oven. She hadn't dressed up exactly, but she looked like she'd made an effort with her hair and make-up.

"I've got some wine," James announced.

"So did I!" replied Lisa, "Put that one in the fridge, I've already opened the other one."

James did as he was told, taking the opened bottle into the living room and pouring them a generous glass each. Lisa came in with a huge bowl of salad and placed it on the table while James searched for some music to put on.

They sat down at the table, and Lisa started to serve the food.

"Thank you for this," James said, smiling at her.

"I thought after the lovely day you gave me today this was the least, I could do to say thank you," she replied.

"And there was me thinking it was because I had just become a multi-millionaire," James said laughing.

"Well, of course, there is that as well," she said, smiling. After a lovely dinner, they shared the washing up, and while Lisa went for the second bottle of wine, James moved the table and chairs back into their usual position. He sat at one end of the sofa whilst Lisa sat at the other end with her back leaning against the arm of the sofa and her feet on his lap. They stayed like this for hours talking, laughing, listening to music, drinking wine and eventually falling asleep. For the second successive night, they slept together on the sofa (fully clothed).

Chapter 7

James awoke on the sofa for the second morning running, Lisa was curled up at the other end still fast asleep. James went to the kitchen and made himself tea. He went to his room and came back to the kitchen sitting at the table, staring at the lottery ticket. *Well, here we go,* he thought to himself as he turned the ticket over and reached for his phone. He read all the details on the back regarding making claims and then having taken a deep breath, he dialled the number on the ticket.

The phone the other end rang three times.

"Good morning, thank you for calling the Camelot claim line, my name is Sarah, how can I help you?"

"Hi Sarah, I think I have the winning lottery ticket for Friday's EuroMillions," James said.

"Thank you, sir, I'll put you through," Sarah said.

The phone rang three times again.

"Hi, this is Paul, how can I help you this morning?"

"Hi Paul, as I was just telling Sarah I think I have the winning ticket for Friday's EuroMillions," James repeated.

"That's great sir, Could I take your name. Please, and what part of the country you are calling from please?" Paul asked.

"My name is James Bolton, and I'm calling from Southeast London."

"Well, that's a good start, sir as we know the winning ticket was sold in Southeast London," Paul informed him.

"Can you confirm the winning numbers please?" Paul asked.

"Certainly," James said. "6, 14, 21, 32 and 46 and the lucky stars are 8 and 11," he told him.

"That's great," said Paul, "Finally, can you give me the 16-digit number on the bottom of the ticket, please?"

"Yes, just a moment, here it is," as James read the numbers, he could feel himself trembling.

"Hold the line one moment please Mr Bolton," said Paul. It felt like forever and then suddenly a voice came on the line.

"Is that James Bolton?" a new voice asked.

"Yes," said James.

"Congratulations James you have the only winning ticket to last Friday's EuroMillions and I am at liberty to inform you that as the holder of that ticket you have won £74,244,962," the voice told him.

"Wow!" was all that James could say.

"I have your mobile number on my screen here. If it's OK, I would like to call you back in ten minutes so we can have a chat?" the voice said. "This is standard procedure," he assured him.

"That would be fine," James replied. "Sorry I didn't catch your name?"

"I'm Alex," he said.

"OK, Alex, I'll talk to you in a few minutes." James hung up. Lisa was standing in the doorway to the kitchen, looking half asleep.

"Who were you talking too?" she asked.

"Camelot," he replied.

"And?" she said.

"I've just won £74 million quid," he said. "Give me a kiss!" Lisa ran out of the kitchen, screaming.

"Where are you going?" James shouted.

"We're not having our first real kiss without me brushing my teeth," she shouted.

"Very good point," he said. "Make room in that bathroom for me!"

They both brushed their teeth and then shared the most sensuous of kisses. It was a totally new experience for them both. She had never kissed a millionaire, and he had never kissed anyone as a millionaire.

As promised, ten minutes later, James phone rang, and he pressed the button to answer it.

"Hello, is that James?" a voice at the other end of the line asked.

"Yes, it is," James replied.

"Great, it's Alex from Camelot here."

"Hi, Alex."

"So, is the news sinking in yet?" he asked.

"Not really, what happens now?" asked James.

"My first question will determine that. Do you want publicity?" he asked.

"Most definitely not," James replied.

"OK, that is your prerogative. We'll need to arrange for somewhere you can get together with our people so we can discuss various aspects of a win this size, what you should do with your money and details of cash management etc," Alex explained. "When will suit you, James?" he asked.

"As soon as possible," he replied. "Is it OK if I bring someone with me?"

"Of course, in fact, we advise it. You will be given a lot of instructions and advice, and it is often better to have someone with you," said Alex.

"OK then, how soon can we do this?" asked James.

"The sooner, the better really," Alex told him. "How about tomorrow?"

"Sounds good to me."

"OK, we have a suite at the Dorchester Hotel. Can you be there at 11:00 am?"

"No problem," replied James.

"OK, bring some ID with you and just ask for Alex Johnson at reception," he said.

"Fine, see you there."

"Lisa, get your glad rags ready, were going to the Dorchester Hotel tomorrow morning," James informed her smiling broadly.

"But James, I've got work," she exclaimed, really upset that she may have to miss out.

"Not now you haven't." he informed her, "I'll cover your day's money," he said. "In fact, I'll give you a job as my PA, and you'll never have to go to work again."

"Hmmm, let's slow down a bit," she laughed. "I'll come tomorrow, but I'm not so sure about the PA thing."

"Well, we can talk about that later, for now, let's just concentrate on tomorrow."

Chapter 8

The Maclaren brothers were out and about on their normal Sunday trip around the local pubs. In and out with their driver left waiting outside for his next destination to be given to him. In each pub, the format was the same, ordering drinks and then a cosy chat with the Landlord. Generally enquiring if they had experienced any problems lately or if there was anything, they could do to help them out. Most landlords declined any help from the brothers as it meant being indebted to them, which was something no-one wanted. One landlord who was so fed up with a group of customers who had recently started using his pub and had suddenly become very difficult to handle took the Maclaren's up on their offer of help. The brothers and some friends turned up a couple of days later and confronted the other gang with the outcome being a huge fight with baseball bats, and pickaxe handles being used as weapons. It had the desired effect in that he never saw the other gang again, but it had cost him a fortune in damages and was still paying the Maclaren's a year later for their services. That kind of muscle didn't come cheap.

On this occasion, after the usual greetings and questions, the brothers seemed to change tack.

"Has anyone been flashing any money around lately?" they asked.

This bought a negative reply from most of the landlords, but a couple of names were put forward which the Maclaren brothers made a note of. But generally, they were not getting any closer to where the money or the lottery ticket had disappeared to. When they reached the Crown, Billy and Jack sent their driver home telling him that they would be able to get a cab from here. They slipped him a few quid and off he went.

They entered the pub which was quite busy and headed for a couple of stools at the end of the bar. They sat and waited patiently as the barmaid served another customer. When she arrived at the end of the bar, Billy ordered two drinks. As she returned with the drinks, Billy took out a note to pay her with. "One for yourself, sweetheart," he added with a smile. She didn't really want to take a drink from them but didn't want to offend them either.

"Thank you," she said, "that's very kind of you."

She went to the till and returned with the change for Billy. "Where's the guvnor?" Jack asked, trying to give her his nicest smile.

"He's just popped out, be back in about 15 minutes," she informed him.

As they sat sipping on their pints, Billy noticed Terry at the other end of the bar and beckoned for him to come and join them. Terry obliged and pulled another stool up to the bar.

"How are you doing Terry?" Billy asked with a smile.

"Yeah, I'm good," Terry replied, feeling a little nervous as he always did when in the company of these two.

"How's work going?" Jack enquired. "We might have a couple of bits and pieces for you to do for us soon," he smiled.

"Just let me know Jack," Terry said.

Terry had got involved with the Maclaren's a couple of years before when he was suffering financial problems due to his gambling. They had asked him to do a couple of jobs for them, and they would straighten things with the bookies he owed. Terry had ended up moving drugs all over the country for them and even once to New York. When his gambling dues had been settled, they kept coming back to him to do more. Admittedly it paid well, but he was still very unsure about it and had never confided in James about his 'second job'. He wanted to tell the Maclaren's that he'd had enough of drug smuggling, but he'd got used to the money, and they were very difficult people to refuse.

The landlord appeared carrying three pints.

"There you go," he said, passing the drinks to them. "On the house."

One thing Terry did like about being with the Maclaren's was that you very rarely paid for anything.

"Any problems Geoff?" Jack asked.

"No, been very quiet," he replied.

"Geoff, have you noticed anyone in here spending a bit more cash than they usually do?" asked Billy.

"Err, no. I don't think so," replied Geoff, glancing quickly at Terry.

"What about you?" he asked, turning to Terry.

"Not that I've noticed Billy," he replied, "Why's that?"

"Just think someone may be spending money around here that isn't necessarily theirs."

"Can't say I've noticed anything Billy, but I'll keep my eyes open."

"There's a drink in it for either of you if you see anything," Jack added.

"OK," they said together.

Terry made his excuses and went back to the other end of the bar and joined James and Gary.

"What are you doing with those guys?" Gary inquired. "Do you know what bad news they are?"

"Yes, but when they invite you to drink with them, you don't say no," Terry replied.

"What did they want?" inquired James.

"Nothing much, they were just looking for someone."

"I wouldn't want to be that person," James said, laughing and looking at Gary who joined in the laughter.

"You certainly wouldn't," Terry agreed.

"One for the road please, Geoff!" Gary called to the landlord.

"I'll get them," James insisted.

Terry and Geoff just looked at each other.

After finishing their pints James and Gary made their farewells and left the pub.

"Geoff!" Terry called, "have you got any of yesterday's papers still lying around?" he asked.

"Maybe, I'll lookout in the office," he said, walking away. He returned a minute later with Saturday's Daily Mirror in his hand and threw it on the bar in front of Terry.

"What do you want that for?" he asked.

"Just to check some racing results," Terry replied.

James arrived home, carrying two bags from the local Chinese takeaway.

"Lisa, I'm home," he called out as he came through the front door. "I've got us Chinese, get some plates out."

Lisa appeared from the living room and rushed into the kitchen.

"I like you having money," she said, laughing.

They sat and ate their food and finished off a bottle of wine from the night before.

"I found your suit and gave it a brush, and I've also washed a couple of your shirts, so you have a choice for the morning," she said.

"Thank you," James replied. "Have you ever been to the Dorchester?" he asked her.

"I went to a reception there once, but I think we were in the cheap part," she laughed.

"Well, from now on it will always be the expensive part," James said.

"Maybe for you, but I'm still going to be skint," Lisa replied. "That's true, perhaps I'll drag you along with me occasionally," laughed James.

Chapter 9

James awoke well before the alarm clock went off. He sat in the kitchen, waiting for the kettle to boil. He made two cups of tea and went to Lisa's room. It was the first night since all this had started that James had actually slept in his own bed and it had felt good except for the fact that he wasn't with Lisa. She had gone off to her room early the previous evening and left James watching TV although his mind was elsewhere.

"Morning honey, a cup of tea here," James said as he entered her room.

Lisa was sitting up in bed, watching the morning news. She smiled and thanked James as she took her tea and placed it on the bedside cabinet.

"Are you excited?" she asked.

"I think I must be; I've been awake for ages."

"So have I," she said.

James went out into the kitchen and sat pensively with his cup of tea. *Well, this is it*, he thought to himself, "take the money, and there's no going back." He had started to get used to the thought of being rich and was very much enjoying it. He had started to think of all the things he wanted to do. He would look after his mum firstly, of that he was sure. Perhaps buy her a new house, somewhere in the country. He could travel the world and never work again. *Oh shit, work*, he thought and reaching for his phone he dialled the number for the metal fabricators he worked at.

The phone kept ringing at the other end and was eventually answered.

"Hi John," he said. "Sorry mate, I won't be in today, in fact, I might not be in for a few days," he continued, "I've got something I need to sort out."

"Oh Shit, Jim," the voice on the other end said, "We'll be right up the shit street without you."

"Sorry mate, but I won't be there, I'll explain later," and with that, he hung up feeling a little guilty but he could live with it. After breakfast, they both got ready and at 9:40 am they left the house to make the short walk to the station.

Both looking very smart they got to the entrance of the station when a voice called out.

"You two getting married or something?" James turned to see Geoff standing in the entrance to the pub laughing. James just laughed, waved and entered the station.

They got the 10:08 am train and just before 10:25 am they were at Victoria Station again. They came out of the station to see rows upon rows of buses and taxis filling up with passengers and trying to make their way to hundreds of different destinations. Having done his homework, James knew what bus they needed and where to catch it. They waited a couple of minutes, and their bus came. In only a few minutes they were alighting from the bus at Hyde Park Corner. They continued walking and followed the road into Park Lane and past the huge gates of Hyde Park. They crossed to the other side of the road, past The Hilton Hotel and continued up until they came to the Dorchester. They entered the palatial reception area, full of hustle and bustle with people coming and going, and they made their way to the reception desk. It was 10:52 am. They were a little early, but James preferred things that way.

"Good Morning," James said to the smartly dressed young man at the desk. "I have an appointment to see Mr Alex Johnson, he has a suite here." James suddenly realised that his best suit was perhaps not quite as smart as he thought it was.

"Ah Yes," said the smart young man as he looked through the diary, "Mr Johnson said he was expecting someone, I'll let him know you have arrived, please take a seat."

James and Lisa took a seat in the reception area and grinned at each other like schoolchildren.

"Fancy getting a room for the night?" James said, laughing. Before Lisa could answer a young lady in a smart blue suit approached them.

"Mr Bolton?" she asked.

"That's me," said James as he got to his feet and shook her hand.

"Lovely to meet you, I'm Candy, I work for Camelot," she introduced herself. She stopped for a moment and looked at Lisa, awaiting an introduction.

"Mrs Bolton?" she ventured.

"Oh sorry, no this is Lisa my, er, best friend," said James, not really knowing how to introduce her.

"Hi," she said. "Please follow me."

James and Lisa did as they were asked and followed Candy across the huge reception to the lifts, she pressed the button, and the lift arrived.

"Fourteen please," Candy said to the lift attendant, and the lift moved smoothly upwards. When they arrived at their floor, Candy led them along a beautifully decorated hallway and then stopped at the end in front of a pair of double doors. She pressed the doorbell, and it opened almost instantly.

"James, please come in," said a voice he vaguely recognised, "Hi, I'm Alex nice to meet you."

"Hi," James replied, "This is my friend, Lisa."

Alex nodded at Lisa in recognition, and she smiled back at him. "Coffee anyone?" Candy asked.

"No thanks," said James and Lisa in unison, both more interested in getting down to business.

"OK then," Alex began, "let's get started, firstly congratulations from everyone here at Camelot, this is one of the biggest wins for a British player, and we want to just explain a few things to you. It goes without saying that this is going to be a life-changing event for you." he smiled at them both. "Firstly, can I have a form of ID and, more importantly, the winning ticket." James opened his wallet and pulled out his driving licence along with the ticket and gave them to Alex, who studied them both carefully.

"You haven't signed the back of the ticket," he said, showing the ticket to James.

"Does that matter?" asked James.

"Not now you're here it doesn't, but if you had dropped this in the street anyone could have picked it up and claimed your prize." James almost blushed. "Anyway, everything seems to be in order. Please take a seat, there's quite a bit of ground for us to cover."

They sat in the luxurious surroundings as Alex explained to them all the things that go with being a lottery winner, the upsides and the downsides. He went on to explain that Camelot had a team of financial advisors who would come and see them and give them sound advice on where to put their money for the best returns. It all sounded very reassuring to James if a little overwhelming.

After about half an hour of detailed and sage advice, Alex asked James for his bank details which James happily disclosed. "One piece of advice that winners seem to find most useful is to take your time deciding what to do with the money. I'm sure there are family members and friends you would like to make gifts to, and our advisors can explain the most effective way to do that. However, we do very much urge you to take a short holiday and get away from your normal surroundings whilst you get used to the idea of being a multi-millionaire. I have a travel agent we can call if you would like me to but take a few moments first to think about where you would like to go."

Lisa looked at James, "Where do you want to go?" she asked.

"I don't know," he replied. "What about you?"

"What?" she said, looking at him inquisitively.

"Well, you're coming as well," he said. "I'm not going on my own!"

Alex laughed, "While you decide who's going and where, let me explain about how we pay you your winnings," he said, getting very business-like again. "It will take a few days to transfer the full amount into your account so as we're speaking Candy is authorising payment of £100,000 into your current account. When you return from your holiday, we will speak to you again about where the rest will be transferred to," he continued, "maybe some into a deposit account etc. Please don't be concerned, this is normal practice. Now then, let's get you a holiday booked. Where do you fancy going?" After a short conversation, James and Lisa decided a week in Lanzarote would be fine for now. As James pointed out, it's not overly exciting, but they show football and sell Carling. He wasn't difficult to please. Alex called his travel agent and got all the details sorted out and informed James that a car would be picking them up the following morning at seven-thirty to take them to Gatwick Airport where the flight tickets and accommodation details would be waiting.

"All there is now is to say bon voyage and to wish you all the best in your new life," said Alex as he shook James warmly by the hand.

"Thank you," James replied, feeling somewhat overwhelmed as everything seemed to come into sharp focus at once. They left the suite and travelled down in the lift to the reception area in numb silence. As they exited the lift, James looked around the reception area.

"Quick this way," he pulled Lisa by the arm across to the other side of the room. Along the wall was a bank of about ten cash machines. Going to the first vacant one James put his card in and entered his PIN code, he pressed the button for balance enquiry and there it was, he had just over £100,000 in his bank account.

"Wow!" he said, "I already feel like a millionaire, and we haven't even scratched the surface. Fancy a drink?" he asked her.

"It's a bit early for a drink, isn't it?" Lisa replied.

"Not today it's not," he said as he strode out looking for the nearest pub.

James and Lisa walked through the backstreets of Mayfair, looking for an open pub. They continued along South Audley Street and past The American Embassy in Grosvenor Square. "Fancy a weekend doing some Christmas shopping in New York?" James asked as they stood looking up at the US Embassy.

"James, I am not in a position to travel the world with you," Lisa said, "I have to work, I have bills to pay."

"I can pay your bills," James offered.

"I think we're getting ahead of ourselves again, James, let's just have a good time and see where things lead us," Lisa said, smiling at him.

"But we…"

"James," she said, interrupting him, "No, buts, let's just wait and see." Lisa slipped her arm through his, and they continued walking without talking.

They got onto Oxford Street, and Lisa's eyes lit up.

"Shall we do some shopping?" she asked excitedly. "You must need some new gear for our week in Lanzarote?"

"And so, must you," James added, smiling.

As Lisa headed for the largest Primark, she had ever seen James pulled her by the arm and further along Oxford Street into Selfridges.

"I have just taken receipt of £100,000, let's treat ourselves." They left Selfridges laden down with bags and continued through the heart of London's shopping area. Stopping here and there to look into the shop windows. They ended up at Oxford Circus and found their way onto Regent Street. After a quick look around Liberty's, they came out to find a small, well-hidden, pub.

"This will do," James said, pushing the door open. They entered a very old-fashioned looking establishment, reassuringly dark with low ceilings. It was quiet when they entered, but James knew as soon as the lunchtime crowd appeared you wouldn't be able to move.

They ordered the drinks and sat at the bar, surrounded by their shopping bags.

"I know I'm stating the bleeding obvious, but this is better than going to work," Lisa said.

As James was about to answer his phone began to ring.

Looking at the display, he saw it was Terry calling him.

"Hello mate, how you are doing?" James asked.

"I'm good," replied Terry. "I popped into your work, they said you had taken the day off, where are you?" he inquired. "Me and Lisa are sitting in a pub in the West End having a drink, we've just been shopping for our holiday," he told him.

"Holiday?" Terry asked, sounding surprised.

"Yes, we're going to Lanzarote tomorrow," said James.

Alarm bells started ringing in Terry's head. He had been worried about James sudden frivolity with cash, but since his conversation with the Maclaren's, he was now more concerned.

"How can you suddenly afford to be shopping in the West End and going on holiday?" he probed.

"I still had some money left from the win on the horse, and we got the holiday really cheap," James replied, suddenly realising he couldn't keep using one winning horse as an excuse. "James, I need to have a serious chat with you mate, can you meet me later?" he asked.

"OK," said James, "I'll meet you in the Crown later."

"No, not in the Crown," Terry said, "meet me in that new pub in the High Street about 3:00 pm."

"See you there," James replied abruptly hanging up the phone. James and Lisa had a few more drinks, did a bit more shopping and despite Lisa's protests regarding the cost they got a taxi all the way home.

It was just coming up to 3:00 pm as they neared home. James dropped Lisa and all the shopping at the house and got the cab to drop him round to the High Street.

Terry was already in the pub when the taxi pulled up. When he saw James getting out and paying the driver, he suddenly felt a palpable sense of foreboding.

"Hiya mate," James said as he entered the bar, "what you having to drink?"

"Just get yourself a drink and come and sit down," said Terry as he walked away from the bar to a secluded corner table.

James, with a drink in hand, followed Terry over to the table and sat down.

"Look, mate," Terry said with a concerned look on his face. "Where the fuck is all this money coming from?"

James looked back at him and said, "I told you, I won it on a horse."

"I don't believe you," Terry said, staring him straight in the eye.

"Why would I lie to you?" James asked.

"I don't know," Terry replied. "But I do know there wasn't a 20/1 winner on Friday, I checked the results."

James' eyes looked down at the table, not quite knowing what to say.

"It may have been a dog," James suddenly said, knowing that his friend was not going to accept that.

"James don't lie to me. Where did the money come from?"

"I don't see what business that is of yours," James replied.

"I just hope to fuck it didn't come from anywhere dodgy James, because questions are being asked."

"If you really want the truth my mother gave it to me," James replied. "She's been ill, and she's worried that if she dies, I will have to pay inheritance tax on it so she has given me some now but made me promise not to tell anyone so the taxman won't find out."

"Really?" asked Terry.

"Honest," James told him.

"I hope to God you're telling me the truth mate. I really do." The two friends changed the subject, had a few more drinks and went for a Curry. James tried to convince himself that that was the end of the matter but, deep down, he knew otherwise.

Chapter 10

James and Lisa had woken early and just as promised a car picked them up at 7:30 am to take them to the airport.

They drove out through the suburbs of South London and onto the motorway. Within twenty minutes they were pulling up outside the Gatwick North terminal for their flight. They made their way to the ticket desk where they were given two tickets and an envelope. The letter inside informed them that a car would be waiting for them at the airport in Lanzarote to take them to their hotel.

They checked-in their luggage, made their way to the security gate and continued on to the departure lounge. After a cursory look around the Duty-Free shop, a call went out for their flight, and they made their way to the gate.

***

The sound of his phone ringing woke Terry. *Shit, I'm late for work,* he thought as he tried to focus on the screen of his phone. He could just about make out the name of Billy Maclaren on his phone. He considered not answering it but knew that was pointless.

"Morning, Billy," he said yawning.

"Terry, we need a meet with you," Billy said more as an instruction than a request.

"Fine Bill, I can meet you after work?" Terry said.

"No Terry, be in the café at 9:30 am." The phone went dead. *Fuck, I really don't need this,* thought Terry.

Terry phoned work to tell them he wouldn't be in and went into the kitchen to make himself tea. He showered and dressed and walked into the café at 9:30 am exactly. Billy and Jack were waiting at a table both devouring huge full English breakfasts.

"Morning, Terry," Billy said with a mouth full of sausage and egg. "Take a seat."

Terry ordered a cup of tea and sat down facing Billy. He smiled at Jack, who just looked at him as he dipped his toast into his fried egg.

"Do you remember I was talking to you the other night about someone throwing money around?" asked Billy.

"Yes," Terry replied.

"Do you have anything to tell me?" he asked, smiling an evil smile that looked even worse with a combination of egg and ketchup coming from the corner of his mouth.

"No," said Terry, "I've heard nothing."

"Strange that, because we've been given some information about someone who has been spending a lot of cash the last few days," continued Billy. "He also just happens to be a mate of yours."

Terry felt the muscles in his stomach start to tighten. "Really?" he said, "and who would that be?" he asked nervously.

"James Bolton," Billy said. "do you know him?" he asked, "and be very careful how you answer, Terry."

"Yes, I do know him," Terry's mouth was getting quite dry now, and as the waiter put his tea down, he immediately picked it up and took a mouthful, trying to disguise that his hand was shaking slightly.

"You never mentioned him to me, did you, Terry?"

"Never thought of it really," said Terry, "he's just a quiet guy who has a couple of beers, he's never been involved in anything dodgy."

"Well, he might be now," growled Jack.

"I'll have a word with him," Terry said.

"Not for a while you won't," said Billy. "He's gone away, my blokes followed him in a chauffeur-driven car down to Gatwick this morning."

"I didn't know that," Terry said, trying to sound convincing. This was not good news, *If they were already tailing him, they must be pretty sure he's involved*, thought Terry.

"Now what I want you to do is contact your mate, wherever he may be, and find out where he's got his new-found wealth from, OK?" ordered Billy.

"I'll get straight on it," Terry replied.

"Make sure you do," Jack emphasised, pointing his knife menacingly at Terry.

"I'll get the next plane if I have to," Terry said. "You know I won't let you guys down; I never have."

"How will you get the next plane, Terry?" Billy asked.

"Simple I'll go to the airport and get a ticket when I get there," he explained.

"Now that's strange," said Billy, in a very calm voice, "when I said he'd gone away you acted surprised, but now you seem to know where he's gone," his voice now not so calm, "are you holding out on me, Terry?"

Terry could feel perspiration beads around his shirt collar as he sat and faced the two hardest men he had ever met in his life. He didn't really know what to say.

"You've gone very quiet, Terry."

"I'll sort it, I promise," Terry said almost pleading with them.

"You make sure you do son," Billy sounded very threatening, "cos next time I see you, I will expect a full explanation of where your mate got his money from."

"OK, Billy, when will I see you?"

"Who knows," said Billy. "By the way, be a good lad and pay the man for our breakfast," he added, smiling as they both left the café.

Terry finished his tea and paid the bill. How the fuck was he going to get in touch with James and what had the idiot done. Surely, he hadn't ripped off the Maclaren's. Surely, he wasn't that stupid?

***

The plane landed at Arrecife Airport about 15 minutes earlier than expected. James and Lisa got off the plane and onto a single-decker bus that was waiting to take the passengers to the terminal. As they drove across the tarmac of the airport, they could see palm trees in the distance.

"This looks great," Lisa said. "I can't wait to get to the hotel and get changed into something more appropriate."

Although it wasn't the height of summer, it was still nearly 80 degrees Fahrenheit, and the sky was a beautiful cloudless blue.

"I think lying by the pool with a nice cold beer could be the plan for today," James replied, smiling.

They got off the bus and entered the pleasantly air-conditioned terminal. They were shepherded towards the passport control, watched closely by police carrying automatic weapons and long faces. Once through the immigration controls, they followed the signs to the baggage collection.

"My luggage is always last off the plane," James told Lisa.

"Perhaps having money changes everything then," smiled Lisa, as she pointed to the carousel and the first two cases coming around were theirs.

They left the baggage reclaim and walked out into the main terminal. There were people everywhere. Everything seemed to be chaotic. As they looked for their driver, an announcement started to play out over the PA system.

"Would a Mr James Bolton recently arrived from London Gatwick please go to the information desk," it announced.

"I bet our car hasn't arrived," James said, rather frustrated. "It can't be that," Lisa replied. "Look," She was pointing at a man standing with a board which read, *JAMES BOLTON,* "That must be our car."

They went over to the man who was holding up James name and explained that they needed to go to the information desk before leaving.

"No problem," the man said in perfect English and loading their cases onto a trolley, "follow me."

They followed him across the terminal, busily trying not to trip over holidaymakers all looking up at the departure boards instead of where they were going.

He stopped at a long counter with the words 'INFORMACION/INFORMATION' in huge letters above it.

A very pretty Spanish girl came over to him, "Can I help you?"

"Yes, please," he said. "An announcement went out asking me to contact information, here I am."

"Very good sir and your name is?" she asked.

"Oh, sorry," he said, "James Bolton."

"Just one moment, sir." She walked to the desk at the back and started going through some of the papers there. She picked one out of the pile and walked back across and placed it in front of James.

"Thank you," he said.

They turned away from the counter, and James removed the piece of paper from the envelope. As he read it, he looked puzzled.

"What is it?" asked Lisa.

"It's a message for me to urgently contact Terry," he said.

"What for?"

"It doesn't say," he replied. "That's very strange, I'll call him when we get to the hotel."

The drive to the hotel took about thirty minutes, and it was certainly worth the wait. The doorman took the cases from the car, and the driver refused to take a fare as he said it was already covered. *Being rich is great,* thought James, *nobody wants paying!*

The hotel reception was sumptuous – not quite the Dorchester but lovely, nonetheless. The reception staff booked them in and called a young man over in a smart suit which must have been very hot if he ever left the artificial chill of the air conditioning. The young man picked up their suitcases and led them to the lift. As they got in, he produced a key from his pocket and placed it in a lock on the control panel. He turned the key, and a light came on at the top of the panel which read penthouse, and he pressed it. The lift climbed very quickly and when it stopped the doors opened directly into one of the most beautiful hotel suites James had ever seen.

"Wow!" said Lisa as she stepped into the room.

The young man walked across the room and opened a door which led into a bedroom. He placed both suitcases onto stands designed for such use.

He came back over to James and gave him a key.

"This is for the elevator," he said, "no one can get up here without one."

"That's great," James replied, foraging through his pocket for some money to tip the young man. He produced a €20 note from his pocket and attempted to give it to him.

"Sorry sir, we do not accept gratuities at this hotel, but it was kind of you to offer."

With that, he was in the lift and gone.

James sat at the desk in the suite and picked up the phone.

The receptionist answered immediately. "Could you get me a number in London, England?"

"Certainly, sir." James gave her the number.

Terry felt his phone vibrating in his pocket. He took the phone out and saw a number he didn't recognise. Normally he would not answer these calls but, on this occasion, he did.

"Hello," he said.

"Hello, sir," a foreign-sounding voice replied, "This is the Condor Resort in Lanzarote, please hold the line I have a call for you."

"Hi Terry, are you there?" said James, "what's going on?" he asked.

"Mate, there's trouble this end, and we need to talk," Terry said. "The Maclaren's seem to think you've ripped them off for a load of money."

"I wouldn't get involved with people like that," James replied.

"I know that, but they've been told that you're flashing cash around and they seem to think it's theirs."

James couldn't for one moment imagine one of the Maclaren brothers dropping an envelope in the street, in fact, he had never even seen any of them walk down the street, they nearly always travelled by car. James looked around him. Seeing Lisa standing on the balcony and the splendour he was surrounded by; he wasn't going to give this up without a fight.

"Terry, I told you where this money came from, and you can tell them if you want," James said, feeling rather brave by virtue of the fact he was so far away from them. "And try and find out what money they're looking for."

"You best be being straight with me mate because I think they might kill me?"

"I'll call you in a couple of days," James said.

"Yeah, enjoy your holiday," Terry replied in a sarcastic tone.

Enjoy your holiday, James thought, *I most certainly will,* and he smiled to himself smugly.

They spent the next few days sunbathing during the day either at the luxurious pool or at the beautiful beach, privately owned by the hotel. Everywhere was waiter service and all-inclusive.

On a couple of evenings, they went into the local town to catch some of the local ambiences, and again on a Saturday so James could catch up with the football.

They came back to the hotel just before seven o'clock on the Saturday evening to change before going for dinner. Lisa was pampering herself in the huge bath whilst James sat watching the TV.

The phone rang, and James crossed the room to the desk and picked it up.

"Hello."

"Hi, is that James."

A vaguely familiar voice the other end said, "Yes."

"It's Alex from Camelot here, I believe you're flying back on Monday, is that correct," he asked.

"Yes," he replied.

"James would you mind coming up to meet with me in Manchester instead of London," he said, "we have done all the paperwork, and the money is ready to go into a new account we've opened on your behalf. All I need is for you to sign a few things and were all sorted," he said.

"I should think that will be fine," said James. At that point, Lisa emerged from the bathroom wrapped in a towel.

"Just one minute," James said to Alex and turning to Lisa explained what Alex had just asked him.

"I need to get back to London really," Lisa said, "but why don't you go to Manchester and I'll see you a couple of days later."

"It will mean getting separate flights home," James told her. "I'm a big girl, I think I'll survive," she said James lifted the phone back to his ear.

"OK, Alex," he said, "I'll fly straight to Manchester, but Lisa needs to go to Gatwick."

"No Problem," Alex replied, "I'll get your flight details sent over to the hotel, bye."

"Bye," James said, hanging up the phone.

By the time James had showered and dressed, Lisa was ready and waiting for him. They left the apartment and walked down to the town where they had seen a very nice-looking Chinese restaurant earlier in the day. They were certainly not disappointed – the food was excellent, as was the service.

"Have you heard any more from Terry?"

"No," said James, "all a fuss about nothing, I presume."

They finished their meal and walked down to the harbour area. There were lots of little bars and restaurants which all looked very inviting. They chose one and entered.

It was very small and neat, with half a dozen tables set for dinner and a small bar at one end. They sat at the bar and ordered some cocktails. The barman, who was obviously English immediately picked up on their accents.

"South Londoners, I presume?" he ventured.

"That's right," James said.

"Me too," the barman replied, "I'm Steve, originally from Camberwell," he told them.

"Just down the road from us," Lisa said.

They continued their conversation with Steve, telling stories about South London and enjoying a few drinks and the hospitality until Lisa suddenly realised the time was getting on. "We'd better get going," she said.

James looked at his watch and decided she was probably right. Steve called them a cab, and twenty minutes later, they were riding up in the elevator to their penthouse. As soon as they got in, Lisa went straight to the master bedroom. She appeared a couple of minutes later wearing just a robe and sat on the sofa. James poured them both a drink and sat next to her. They chatted for a few minutes, and as they did, James managed to slide his arm across the back of the sofa and let it fall over her shoulders. She turned to look at him.

"That was a lovely evening," she whispered. "In fact, it's been a wonderful week."

James leaned towards her, and their lips met. Her lips felt so soft against his, and he never wanted this moment to end. But in an instant, she pulled back and looked him in the eyes.

"Thank you," she said.

"For the kiss?" he asked, smiling.

"Well yes, but for everything really, it has been such a wonderful week I don't ever want it to end."

"It doesn't have to," he said, "we have years ahead of us and millions to spend," he added.

"No, you have millions to spend," she corrected him.

"I would happily let you help me spend it," he explained, "there is far too much for me to spend on my own."

Lisa sighed and looked dreamily into his eyes. They sat in silence for a moment, and then Lisa leaned forward and kissed James again.

"It's very late," she said, "bedtime," she stood up and walked towards the master bedroom. James followed her, and as she got to the door, she turned to him. "Good night," she said and closed the door behind her.

James stood in silence for a moment and then turned away, feeling somewhat crestfallen. Recovering his senses, he finished his drink and went to the smaller bedroom as he had every night since they had been there.

It was a beautiful Sunday morning in the Canary Islands, and James and Lisa were lounging by the pool. It had been a blissful few days, and they were due to travel back the following day. The weather, the food and the sunshine had been magnificent. Faultless. The only dark cloud was the lovemaking. There hadn't been any. Yes, they had some very close moments and long sensuous kisses, but still, it hadn't developed any further. The sense of being unfulfilled loomed large. James had naturally concluded that Lisa just didn't find him attractive in that way, however, he couldn't have been any further from the truth. Lisa had repeatedly gone over in her mind how wonderful it would be for James to take her in his arms, and after undressing her make passionate love to her for hours. However, she had been wrestling with a problem. All the time they had known each other, she had been attracted to him in every sense of the word but had never been able to show it. How would it look now he's a multi-millionaire if she's suddenly ready to jump into bed with him?

Chapter 11

It was a Sunday when they came calling. Terry was having a quiet pint with Gary in the Crown when the door opened, and Billy Maclaren walked in with a couple of his henchmen. Gary, who by now knew some of what had been occurring, raised his eyebrows and gestured towards the door as they walked in purposefully. Terry turned towards the door and saw Billy smiling at him. He raised his glass and smiled back. Billy and his guys sat at the other end of the bar and ordered a drink. Terry carried on chatting to Gary, trying to pretend all was ok. But after about fifteen minutes one of Billy's guys inevitably walked the length the bar to Terry and very quietly said, "Mr Maclaren would like a word with you, follow me." As Terry went to move Gary tugged at his sleeve. "Do you want me to come with you?" he asked.

"Thanks, but there's no sense in us both getting battered," Terry replied.

As they got nearer to where Billy sat, he got off his barstool and started towards the door. His man followed him outside with Terry following behind.

Once outside, Billy turned to Terry.

"OK, what do you have to tell me?" he barked.

"I've spoken to him, and he says his mum gave him the money."

"Really?" Billy looked him straight in the eye, and at this moment, Terry realised that it didn't sound very convincing.

"His dear old mum gave it to him?"

"That's what he told me," Terry repeated.

"Is she a wealthy woman then?"

"Not especially," Terry replied, wondering where this line of enquiry was going.

"Well, I had a friend of mine check your mate's bank account, and he's got nearly One Hundred Thousand big ones in there," he said. "Is that from Mummy?"

"I've got no idea," Terry said, genuinely surprised.

"Now I think you know a lot more than your telling me son, I'm starting to think that you may be in on this with him," he said, "As you know, I'm a fair man so here's what I'm going to do, I'm going to give you one more chance to tell me what you know?" his eyes were almost glazing over with rage, "where's my fucking money you thieving little cunt."

"I honestly don't know Billy."

With that Billy just nodded at his two guys and they dragged Terry down the alley that ran alongside the pub. He saw the first blow coming but only realised there was a knuckle duster attached as it landed. The next few blows came to the body, and he felt himself going down. Once on the floor, he could feel kicks raining down on him. After a while, he felt nothing and the next thing he knew Gary was trying to lift him off the floor. He could hear voices around him, but he couldn't see anything.

"Leave him on the floor," said one voice.

"Wait for the ambulance," pleaded another.

He felt himself drift into unconsciousness.

Gary had been at the hospital ever since Terry had been brought in 14 hours ago. He was in a coma and completely nonresponsive.

Despite his best efforts, he'd not been able to get hold of James to find out the full story of what was going on but had been told that Maclaren's men were all over the manor asking questions.

**

Mrs Bolton was sitting in her kitchen watching TV. She did a lot of that these days. Eileen was 64 years old and had lived alone since James had left six years ago. She was very proud of her youngest son, he had never caused her a moment's bother, and he kept in touch calling her at least twice a week. "It was strange," she reflected that she hadn't spoken to him this week.

Since her husband had died five years ago, she had stopped working and lived off a small pension and some secret money that he had stashed away for her. She hadn't even known about the money until after his death when a couple of his pals turned up and handed her a briefcase stuffed with cash which he had been saving for her in case anything should happen to him. She had often wondered how he had saved up so much money, over £30,000, but he wasn't around to ask, so she hid it in lots of different places around the house and used it as and when she needed it.

Her biggest disappointment in life was her eldest son Robert, or Bobby as everyone now knew him. He had left home at the age of sixteen after a huge argument with his father, and apart from her husband's funeral, she had never seen him since. She always got birthday and Christmas cards from him, but that was it. She knew he was very much like his dad, and according to what she had heard, he had quite a few fingers in quite a few pies these days and was doing pretty well for himself. She didn't know exactly what he did, and she didn't really want to know.

It was about ten-thirty when she heard the doorbell ring. She wasn't expecting anyone but the neighbours quite often knocked and popped in for a cup of tea. She got up from the table and walked down the hallway to the door.

"Who is it?" she asked.

"Hi, I'm a friend of your son, and I just need a quick word," the voice answered from the other side of the door.

Eileen put the chain on the door and opened it just the few inches the security chain would allow. She could see two very large men dressed very smartly in suits standing there.

"What do you want?" she asked through the crack in the door.

"It's about your son" one of the men whispered.

"What about him?" Eileen had had heavies like this looking for Robert before even though he hadn't been here for years.

"Mrs Bolton, it would be much easier if we could come in and talk," the other man pleaded.

"Well I'm afraid you can't, I've got some friends here you see."

"OK," the first man said, "your son appears to have come into a rather large sum of money, and we have been led to believe you gave it to him, is this true."

"I wish I had a large sum of money to give to someone, but I haven't, and I certainly wouldn't give it to him even if I had," she answered. "Anyway, what's it got to do with you, are you the police or something?"

The two men looked at each other and said nothing.

"No, I thought not," she said, "go on, piss off before I call them," and with that, she slammed the door abruptly.

Eileen went back into her kitchen and sat down her hands were still shaking when she heard another knock on the door. She remained sitting in her chair, listening intently.

"Eileen, Eileen it's me, Jane," a voice called, "are you, all right, love?"

Eileen rose from her seat and went to the front door.

"They've gone," Jane said.

Eileen opened the door and ushered her friend in. Before closing the door, Eileen had a look right and left to satisfy herself that they had gone.

"Are you OK?" Jane asked as she put the kettle on. "I didn't like the look of them at all."

"Yes, I'm fine," Eileen answered.

"What are you doing here, anyway?" she asked her neighbour. "Well I saw them come to your door," she said, "and I had a feeling they were up to no good," she explained, "and that's when I saw him sitting in the car."

"Who exactly?" asked Eileen.

"That bloody Jack Maclaren," she answered.

"Oh my god," said Eileen, "what is Robert doing getting mixed up with them for?"

"Is that who they were looking for then, your Robert?" she asked.

"Yes, they were asking me questions about some money he told them that I had given him," she explained.

"And did you?" Jane inquired.

"Of course, I didn't. For one I haven't got any money, and secondly, I wouldn't give it to him even if I did."

"He must be in a lot of trouble if they're coming around here looking for him," Jane said, stating the obvious.

"Well, I know that," Eileen snapped back at her.

"I know it's been a long time, Eileen but I do think you should try and get hold of him and warn him," Jane suggested. "I wouldn't know where to start," Eileen sighed despondently. "I could give my Kenny a ring, see if he knows where he is these days if you want?" she offered.

"Yeah, that might work," said Eileen "Oh, by the way, how is your Kenny?" she asked, "I heard he was in the hospital."

"He's OK," said Jane "Just got a bit of a bang on the head, did it at work apparently."

Later that evening Jane was back at home watching TV. When the adverts came on, she reached for the phone and dialled her son's number. After a few rings, he answered. "Hi, Mum," he said, "how you are doing?"

"I'm fine thanks, Kenny, how about you?"

"Had my stitches out today, I'm all on the mend now," he told her.

"Good," she said, "Kenny, I need a favour, you remember your old mate Bobby Bolton. I think he's in trouble."

"Really, what's he done," Kenny asked.

"I'm not sure, but Jack Maclaren turned up at Mrs Bolton's house earlier with a couple of his heavies, and they were a bit threatening," she said. "They were asking about some money that Bobby had and trying to find out where he got it from."

"They threatened Mrs Bolton?" Kenny said in astonishment.

"Well sort of, certainly shook her up a bit," Jane told him "I'll let Bobby know tonight. We'll sort it," he said, "tell her not to worry."

Chapter 12

James was in the bathroom when he heard the phone in their penthouse suite ringing.

"Grab that, please, Lisa," he called out.

"Got it," she called back.

James heard Lisa have a very brief conversation with someone and then return the handset to its cradle.

"That was reception," she called to him, "the boys on his way up for our cases."

"OK, I'm on my way."

James finished brushing his teeth, put the last of his toiletries into the bag and zipped it up. As he left the bathroom, Lisa was standing in the middle of their beautiful suite.

"I just wanted one last look," she said mimicking a sad face.

"I'll tell you what I'll book it again in six-months-time."

As he said it, he picked up the phone and got through to reception.

"Hello, how can I help," the receptionist asked.

"Mr Bolton in the penthouse here," he said, "I would like to book the same suite for the first weekend in March next year, please."

"Just one moment, sir," as James waited, the boy turned up to collect the cases.

"OK, Mr Bolton that is booked for the third of March 2017."

"Third of March, that's great, I'll give you my credit card details on the way out."

As they entered the lift, Lisa turned and looked at James.

"That's the weekend of my birthday."

"Is it really," said James with a knowing smile.

They walked across the reception area, and while James sorted out the reservation for their next stay, Lisa took the opportunity to thank any members of staff she could find for looking after them so wonderfully during their all too brief stay.

As they walked out of the main doors, their car was waiting for them with their luggage already in the boot.

They set off for the airport.

Upon their arrival at Arrecife Airport, they made their way to the information desk.

"Morning," said the young lady at the desk.

"Morning," replied James. "I'm here to pick up a ticket to Manchester in the name of James Bolton."

"Just one moment, sir," she went to the desk at the back and opened the draw after a moment she took out an envelope and removed the contents. She returned to the desk where James was waiting.

"There you are, sir," she said, handing him the ticket. James took a quick look at the ticket and saw that he had over an hour before he had to check-in.

"Shall we get a coffee?" he asked Lisa.

"I've only got half an hour until my gate closes," she said, "better be quick."

They decided to check in her luggage first and then went to buy coffee.

"Thank you so much for a lovely time," she said. "The pleasure was all mine Lisa," he said.

"How long will you be in Manchester?" she inquired. "Only one night," he said. "I'll be back tomorrow. Will you wait for me?" he laughed.

"Well, who knows?" Lisa replied, smiling.

They walked over to the departure gate, and Lisa showed her boarding pass. She turned and kissed James.

"See you tomorrow," she said.

"Bye."

As Lisa walked away, James watched her intently. "I love you," he whispered very quietly to himself.

James boarded his plane an hour later.

They took off for the four-hour flight, and he decided to try and get some sleep. The seat was extremely uncomfortable, and the passengers in front of him had two children under the age of six, so he decided that sleep was probably not an option. Despite shifting around repeatedly, his efforts were futile. After reading some mind-numbingly boring magazines, they eventually made the announcement that they would be landing in approximately thirty minutes.

Despite the children in front of him now getting even louder and more excited, the time had passed fairly quickly. Before he knew it, they were on the ground and taxiing towards the terminal.

Once off the plane, James quickly passed most of the other passengers and through passport control. He arrived at the baggage reclaim carousel before any of the other passengers.

Unlike when he had landed in Lanzarote, this time, he waited for what seemed like an age for his case to come through. When it eventually did, he put it onto a trolley and made his way out into the main terminal building.

As he came into the glare of the public area, he could see a mass of people searching out their friends and loved ones. Standing alone at the far end was the friendly face of Alex Johnson. James walked over towards him, and Alex extended his right hand. The two men shook hands.

"Hi, James, nice holiday?" he asked.

"Lovely," James replied, "and looking forward to plenty more now."

Alex laughed. "I have a car waiting outside for us," he said. "I thought perhaps we could grab some lunch before we go to the office if that suits you."

"Sounds great to me."

They left the terminal and walked to the pick-up area where a large Mercedes was waiting to take them into town. The drive through Manchester took forever. As in most major cities in England, the traffic was virtually gridlocked. On the way, Alex made a couple of phone calls, and it appeared that someone else would be meeting them for lunch.

***

Eileen was carrying out her normal morning ritual of a cup of tea, two biscuits and a bit of daytime TV when the doorbell sounded. After the events of yesterday, she suddenly felt very nervous. She looked down the hallway and could see the silhouette of a large man through the frosted window. She moved closer to the door.

"Go away, or I will call the police," she shouted.

"Open the door Mum, it's me, Bobby," came a voice from the other side of the door.

Eileen nearly ran the last few steps and flung the door open. Standing there, looking a million dollars was her Robert. She embraced him and pulled him through the door.

"Robert, I've been so worried about you," she said, "What's going on?" she asked.

Before he could answer, she darted into the living room and opened the curtain just enough for her to be able to see outside.

"Robert, come here," she called, "There's been a car with two men in it been parked over the road all morning."

"Don't worry, Mum they work for me," he said. "They're here to keep an eye on you."

They walked into the kitchen, and Bobby sat down whilst Eileen put the kettle on.

"Tea?" she asked. "Still take two sugars?"

"Yes, please, Mum," he answered.

"Where have you been all these years?" she asked, "I've not heard from you since your father died five years ago."

"I know Mum, and I'm sorry," he said. "I didn't think you or James deserved to be involved in anything I do these days and it was perhaps better just keeping away."

"Well, you look good, that suit must have cost a nice few quid," she said.

"Money is not a problem," Bobby answered modestly.

When Bobby had left home, he was taken under the wing by a man called Teddy, who was in the protection business. Bobby did little jobs, ran errands and once he learned to drive and got a licence, he became Teddy's driver. He followed Teddy everywhere and listened and learned. He started going out with some of the more experienced guys collecting money and threatening potential new clients came easy to him. By the time he was in his early twenties, he had become Teddy's, right-hand man. He had become very handy with his fists or anything else he could lay his hands on if required. Teddy's business was mainly carried out in North London, and Bobby had by now come to think of the other side of the water as home. He only kept in touch with a few of his old friends from the South but liked to keep himself informed of what was going on.

When Teddy had retired a few years ago, Bobby took on all of his business having to go to work hard to stop other mobs trying to muscle in on his clients.

He had been arrested on numerous occasions, but due to his contacts and money had never been convicted. Bobby was not a man to be messed with.

"So, Mum, tell me what happened with these blokes who came round here?" he asked.

"Well, they knocked on the door and started saying you had some money and had told them I gave it to you," she said, "I told them that I had no money to give anyone and that I was going to call the police if they didn't leave."

"How do you know it was something to do with this Maclaren fella?" he asked.

"Jane saw him in the car," she replied. "You shouldn't get involved with that lot they're pure evil."

"Mum, for one, I haven't got anything that belongs to them, and secondly, believe me, I can handle the Maclarens," he told her.

"Well if this is nothing to do with you, why have they come here?" she asked.

Before her son could answer, a terrible thought occurred to her.

"Oh Robert," she said, "it couldn't be James, could it?" she asked.

"It couldn't be," he replied, "I haven't seen him, but I do keep in touch with people to make sure you and him are OK. From what I know it appears he's just living a quiet life, certainly not mixing with the likes of this Maclaren scum."

"Let me make some discreet enquiries," he reassured her.

Passing her a piece of paper, he said, "This is my number if you see anyone that you're worried about, call me and I'll be here," he assured her. "I'll keep my guys close by just in case."

"OK," she said, "when will I see you again?" she asked, "I'll be around tomorrow, Mum," he said, "I promise," he added as he kissed her on the cheek.

When he left the house, he had a good look around him all he could see that looked out of the ordinary was a black BMW parked up with two big guys in it. He walked over to the car as he got closer the driver's window came down.

"Hi, Razor," Bobby said to the man in the driver's seat. "How's it going?"

"All quiet here," he replied.

Razor Richards was one of Bobby's oldest and most trusted friends. He got the name Razor due to his skilful deployment of the weapon. Many a man walked around London carrying scars that had been inflicted due to his expertise. He could be a nasty and ruthless bastard at times. He once beat a man unconscious in a pub simply because the man had referred to him as 'son'. When Bobby had taken over the business, Razor became his right-hand man and had displayed a loyalty that was second to none. Whenever the going got tough Razor was always by his side.

"OK," Bobby said, "I'm getting someone else down to keep an eye on Mum, I need you to come with me."

Bobby dialled a number into his phone and hit the green button. After a five-minute chat, he came back over to the car "OK, Razor, you're with me know," he said. Looking over to the guy in the passenger seat, he said, "George is on his way down to meet you, any problems call me immediately," he told him.

"Will do Bobby," the man replied.

Bobby and Razor walked over to Bobby's Range Rover, got in and drove away.

"Looks like this is nothing to do with me," he told Razor, "I think it must be my brother," he added.

"Brother?" Razor enquired, "I didn't know you had a brother."

"Yeah," said Bobby. "He's a few years younger than me and straight as a die, I just can't imagine how he's got mixed up with these scumbags."

"Well, what has he done?" asked Razor.

"I'm not sure, to be honest," Bobby replied, "but they seem to think he has some of their money and we need to find him before they do," he continued.

"Where does he live?" Razor inquired.

"Out towards Croydon," Bobby said, "there are a couple of pubs that I know he uses, so we'll try them first."

***

The Mercedes pulled up outside a very flash looking Italian restaurant in the centre of Manchester and before James could move his door had been opened. He got out and waited for Alex to come around from the other side of the car before following him inside.

The Maitre'd welcomed them.

"Hello, Mr Johnson," he said, "I've saved your usual table."

The two men followed him into an exquisitely decorated eating area and to a table in the corner were another man already sat.

"Hello, Martin," said Alex, "please meet James."

Martin rose and shook James by the hand, and then all three men took their places at the table. After a bit of small talk, they ordered lunch and Alex decided it was time to get down to business.

"Martin is to be your personal financial advisor James," Alex informed him, "he will be available to give you advice from this day onward, any questions you may have about your money or investments etc. you can call him."

Martin passed James a business card across the table. "We have taken the liberty of opening a new bank account in your name James," he said.

"What's wrong with the one that I have now?" James asked.

"Certain accounts are designed for the sort of money you now have at your disposal James," he explained, "an ordinary current account is not designed to hold that sort of cash and most high street banks don't like to take risks with the sort of money you have."

"You can transfer some funds into your current account as you wish but remember if a bank goes bust, you're only guaranteed insurance is for £75,000. The bank we have put your money in is a lot safer," explained Alex.

"OK," said James, "that's fine, you know better than I about these things."

"So here are your new account details, James," said Martin, sliding a folder over towards him, "and there is a statement included."

James opened the folder and looked through the papers. When he found the statement, he just sat and stared at it. He had never seen a number that big before in his life. An involuntary smile appeared on his face, and warm glow enveloped him.

"That looks fine," James said.

At this point, the waiter arrived balancing three plates in his hand and served each of them their desired meal.

After they finished eating the three men left and got back into the swish Mercedes. James reflected that he might buy one for himself. They drove for about five minutes before pulling up outside a large office block. They got out and went into a rather sparsely decorated foyer and into a lift to the fourth floor.

They entered an office where James signed all the required paperwork. The exercise seemed so perfunctory, but he was now a seriously rich man.

"I've booked you into a hotel in the city centre," Alex told him, "and there will be a car at your disposal all evening if you require it."

"Think I'll probably be having a few beers and an early night," James said.

Their business concluded, James said his farewells and left. As promised, a car was waiting for him and took him to the Malmaison Hotel in the centre of town. This was the type of luxury to which he was becoming easily accustomed. He booked in went to his room and lay on the bed. Going through his jacket, he removed his phone from the pocket and suddenly realised that it was still turned off. He pressed the power button and after playing a short but very annoying jingle his phone burst back to life.

His first call was to Lisa to make sure she had got home, all right. He dialled the number, but it went straight to answerphone. *She's probably knackered as well*, he thought. He then tried to call Terry again to no avail.

He reached for the remote control for the TV and pressed the on button. As he did, his phone started ringing, it was Gary.

"Hello mate, how are you?" James enquired.

"Where the fuck are you?" Gary shouted exasperated.

"I'm in Manchester," he replied, "why?"

"Well, I'm at the fucking hospital with Terry."

"What's the matter with Terry?" enquired James, suddenly concerned.

"He's in a coma James, the fucking Maclarens gave him a proper hiding over something you've done," the anger rising in his voice.

"I've had nothing to do with the Maclarens," James insisted.

"Well, they seem to disagree," Gary told him.

"OK," James said, "I'm coming home. I'll be there as soon as I can."

"James don't go to your house in case they're looking for you," Gary begged.

"OK, point taken," James replied his calm tone masking the rising sense of panic taking hold.

***

Lisa had had an uneventful flight back to Gatwick. After landing, she went to the train station and got the Gatwick Express. Thirty-five minutes later, she was getting off the train and walking back home, pulling her suitcase behind her. As she passed the pub, Geoff was outside having a cigarette.

"Hi Lisa," he called, "have you seen James?" he asked.

"Yes, why?"

"It's all been going on here lately," he told her, "Terry got badly beaten up the other night, and I had some bloke in yesterday looking for James." Geoff pulled his wallet out from his back pocket and started going through it. "Here you are I've got a number for him." He opened the piece of paper and started to read it. "Bobby is his name; I think he said he was James's brother."

"I wasn't aware he had a brother," Lisa said, looking at the piece of paper Geoff had given her, "anyway I'll see he gets it."

She folded the paper and put it in her pocket and continued to walk. As she did, she took out her phone and tried to call him, but James phone was still switched off.

As she approached the house, she noticed the curtains were drawn in the living room. "That's strange," she muttered.

She approached the front door, paused and rummaged through her handbag for her key. She pushed the key into the lock and opening the door she put her suitcase in first, entered and closed the door behind her.

The house was in darkness, she opened the door to the living room and turned on the light. To her amazement, two men were sitting there dressed in smart suits – one sitting on her sofa and the other reclining languidly in the armchair.

"Where's lover boy then?" the larger of the two asked. Even sitting down, his presence was imposing. As she stood rooted, she suddenly remembered that these were the two guys who had been in the pub the other night who kept staring at her. "I don't know who you mean," she said, "and what are you doing in my house?" she demanded.

"We're looking for James," he said, "we know he didn't get off the plane with you so, where is he?"

"I don't know," she said, "but if you don't get out of my house, I'm going to call the police."

Suddenly she was aware that there was a third man and he was behind her. She felt a hand come around and cover her mouth, and there was an awful acrid smell.

That was all she remembered.

Chapter 13

Fifteen minutes after speaking to Gary, James was in a taxi heading for Manchester Piccadilly Train Station. On his arrival, he almost ran across the concourse to the ticket office. The station was full of afternoon commuters milling around, some checking the time of their trains and others waiting for incoming passengers. James rushed past them all as though they weren't there. When he managed to get to the front of the queue at the ticket office, he asked for a one-way ticket to London Euston. The ticket clerk duly obliged, the ticket shot out of the machine and appeared before him just the other side of the glass petition. He quickly passed his credit card under the glass and took the ticket. With the transaction completed, James was on his way, checking all the information boards for the time of the next London train.

"Platform 7 leaving in ten minutes," a member of the station staff informed him.

"Thanks," said James rushing towards the platform.

Once seated on the train and his suitcase secured into the rack, he attempted to relax, and his thoughts turned to Lisa. He removed his phone from his pocket and dialled her number and again went straight to answer the phone.

A pang of concern seared through him.

The journey was a boring and slow affair. He kept wondering why the Maclarens were so badly on his case and what on earth was he going to do to shake them. They had no proof that the money or the lottery ticket belonged to them, but it was becoming clear to him that they had been the previous owner of both. James was already starting to get used to being rich. He had tasted the high life and was taking to it like a duck to water. He really did not want to give it back, especially to scum like them.

They were already rich and had bullied and stolen for everything they had. No, this was his now, and he was determined to find a way of keeping it. James phoned Gary and told him he was on his way back to London heading straight to the hospital.

He tried to phone Lisa again. Still no answer.

James suddenly remembered he hadn't spoken to his mum. He hit the speed dial on his phone and went directly through to her. After two rings, she answered.

"Hello," Eileen said.

"Hi, Mum, it's me," said James.

"James, I've been so worried," she said, "where have you been?" she asked.

"I decided to have a holiday," he told her. "I've been in Lanzarote for a week."

"I've had people around here looking for you," she said.

"Who?"

"Those Maclaren brothers," she told him.

His heart nearly stopped when he heard this. "Are you OK, Mum?" he asked.

"I'm fine, but they say you've got their money, what's going on?"

"Nothing Mum, I'll get it sorted, just don't open your door to anybody," he told her. "I'll be around later."

"I'll be OK," Eileen said, "your brother has left two of his friends sitting outside the house watching out for me."

"Robert?" he asked.

"Yes," she said. She explained that she had managed to contact his brother and he'd been round to see her and that he was trying to find out what was going on.

"Have you got a phone number for him?" James asked.

"Yes," she replied. James scrambled through his pockets, looking for a pen and some paper which he found.

"OK, give me the number."

Eileen gave James the number, and after promising he would get back to her very soon, he hung up.

James couldn't believe he was about to speak to his big brother again after all these years. He had heard lots of rumours regarding his brother's business and reputation but had refrained from telling people that they were related. James dialled the number his mother had given him. A rather rough voice answered.

"Hello?"

"Hello," James said, "Robert?"

"That can only be one person," Bobby replied, "no one else would dare call me Robert. Hello James," he said.

"Well, what should I call you?" James said, laughing.

"Bobby," he answered.

"OK, Bobby, I hear you've seen Mum?"

"Yes," he replied, "and now I want to know what the fuck you've been up to," he asked.

Without hesitation, James spilled the whole story to his big brother, and it actually felt great to tell somebody else and share the burden. The sense of relief was comforting.

"Fucking hell, seventy-four million quid," he exclaimed, "when you rip someone off you don't fuck about do you, little brother," he said laughing. "Well, let me tell you," Bobby continued, "a crowd of shits like those Maclarens don't fucking deserve to get their hands on that sort of dough, so I am going to help you keep it," he said. "In exchange, you are going to look after Mum and get her moved somewhere nice." "A small contribution to your brother's retirement fund wouldn't go amiss either."

"You can have whatever you want," James said, finally feeling a bit safer.

"Where are you now?" Bobby asked.

"I'm on a train from Manchester," he told him, "I'll be at Euston in about an hour."

"OK, I'll be waiting for you there," Bobby said.

"Will I recognise you?" James asked.

"It's OK, I'll recognise you, little brother," he laughed, "you'll be the one that reeks of money."

James hung up the phone with a smile on his face. He didn't know his brother anymore but felt confident that he knew what he was doing.

James tried to phone Lisa again. Answerphone.

The train pulled into Euston station exactly on time. James retrieved his suitcase and stepped down onto the platform. He strode purposefully towards the main concourse quite excited about seeing his brother. He would have to make a point of remembering to call him Bobby.

As he walked through the gates, he saw Bobby waiting for him. He hadn't changed much but had bulked out into a very big man. He waved towards his big brother who walked towards him.

They embraced in what could only be described as a geezer's hug. As they let go of each other, Bobby quickly said to James, "Who else knows you were in Manchester?"

"Only Lisa," James replied.

"Who's Lisa?" Bobby asked.

"She's my flatmate," said James.

"OK, so no one will be expecting you to get off this train then?"

"I wouldn't have thought so," said James becoming a bit bemused.

"OK, let's get going then," said Bobby.

They walked out of the station and crossed the road to where a Range Rover was waiting, and they both got in.

"James, this is Razor," Bobby said, introducing him to their driver.

"Hi," said James feeling a little nervous just due to the name.

"All right, son," Razor replied.

"I need to go and see Terry," James said, "he's in St George's Hospital."

"You're not going anywhere near him," said Bobby, "they know he's there and they'll have people there looking for you. I've sent two of my blokes over there to keep an eye on things," he assured his brother.

"They obviously think he's involved in this, but I've got a plan to keep him safe," he continued, "but it's going to cost you a few quid."

"Not a problem," said James, "as long as he and Gary are safe."

"OK, phone Gary and tell him to start getting all of Terry's belongings together without making it too obvious and tell him one of my blokes will be in contact with him shortly." James relayed the message to Gary whilst Bobby got on the phone to whoever his contacts may be.

Thirty-five minutes later, an ambulance from a private hospital followed a black Jaguar car into the hospital grounds.

They parked up, and the ambulance men removed a wheeled stretcher from the back of the vehicle and followed the driver of the Jaguar, a very well-presented man in a dark grey suit and carrying a briefcase, into the main entrance of the hospital. The suited man walked up to the main reception. "Excuse me," he said to the receptionist, "my name is Joseph Alexander, and I am a solicitor acting on behalf of one of your patients, Terry Alleyne," he informed her. "I am here with an ambulance to remove him to a private hospital."

Forty minutes later and after a conversation with one of the hospital administrators, Terry was transferred into the ambulance and along with Gary was speeding off to a private hospital with strict instructions to the hospital staff not to disclose any information to anyone.

James, Bobby and Razor were already waiting at the private hospital when the ambulance arrived. The Jaguar pulled up at the front of the building and, as the solicitor got out, Bobby walked straight over to him and shook his hand.

"Thanks for that Joseph, any problems?" he asked.

"No, it went like clockwork," he answered.

"No one followed you?"

"I checked my mirrors all the way, there was no one," the solicitor replied.

"Thanks again," said Bobby.

The solicitor went back to his car and drove away.

Bobby came back into the reception area where James was waiting.

"This is someplace," James said, "how much is this costing me?" he asked.

"Ooh, about a grand a night I should think."

"Wow!" said James.

"You can fucking afford it," Bobby laughed.

"That's true," James replied.

Gary appeared in the reception and came straight over to where James and Bobby were sitting.

"Gary, meet my brother Bobby," said James. The two men shook hands.

"What the fuck is going on?" he asked James.

"It's a long story but rest assured we will be OK now," said James.

"And who the fuck is paying for this place?" he asked.

"You're not going to believe this, but I am," James said.

"So, you have ripped the Maclarens off," Gary said.

"Not exactly," replied James, "but when this is all over, there will be a nice few quid in it for everyone."

"For now," Bobby interjected, "do not tell anyone about this place or anything else you know even to Terry's family. If you feel unsafe, I'm sure James will be able to send you on holiday until everything blows over."

"I'd rather stay here and help sort out the bastards who did this to Terry," said Gary.

"You're more than welcome," Bobby said, "but my sense is that it's going to get very nasty."

"I'm up for it," said Gary, although he realised, he was probably getting in way above his head.

"Good man," Bobby said, "what I want you to do for now is stand guard over Terry. Razor will take you home to get some clothes and bits, and you can sleep in one of the guest rooms here. There will be two guys outside the hospital at all times, and I'll give you a phone number for them," he continued, "just in case anyone somehow slips past them."

"OK," Gary said.

Gary and Razor left, and James and Bobby were shown to Terry's room by a doctor.

"So, what's the situation then, Doctor?" James asked.

"He's still in a coma," the doctor said, "but he is responding to stimuli so I think he might regain consciousness soon. He's not out of the woods yet though."

James and Bobby went into the room and sat down looking at Terry was lying perfectly still with tubes coming from everywhere. "So, tell me about this Lisa then, is she more than a flatmate?" asked Bobby.

"Hopefully," James said, smiling. "That has just reminded me I must try and call her again."

He rang her number again; it went straight to answerphone.

"That's strange," James said.

"What is it?" asked Bobby.

"I've been trying to get hold of Lisa all day," he told his brother, "and her phone has been off."

"Where is she and why the fuck didn't you mention this before?" asked Bobby looking a bit panicked.

"She flew back from Lanzarote this morning and was going straight home," James said.

"Oh, fuck," said Bobby, "quickly, give me your address." He was already dialling a number on his phone.

"Frank, its Bobby," he said, "I need you to go and check an address out for me."

As James told him the address, Bobby repeated it over the phone.

"Get around there and get inside, even if you have to break in," he told him.

James was turning very pale in the face.

92

Chapter 14

Frank turned up at James and Lisa's house at 11:15 pm, and it was shrouded in darkness. He left his companion at the garden gate and walked up to the front door. He knocked loudly and got no response, he walked along the front of the house to see if he could make anything out through the windows, but the curtains obscured any view at all.

"I'll have to break in," he whispered to his comrade, "is there anyone about?"

"No," the other man mouthed back.

Frank removed a small cosh from his pocket and turning his face away he smashed the small pane of glass in the front door. He then squeezed his arm through and reached down to turn the handle on the inside. He eased open the door. As he stepped inside, he could see a woman's handbag lying on the floor in the hallway. He moved slowly into the living room and, on the table, he glimpsed a mobile phone and a note:

IF YOU WANT TO SEE HER ALIVE TAKE THIS PHONE AND DIAL 1 ON THE SPEED DIAL. I AM COMING FOR MY MONEY, YOU WILL NOT ESCAPE FROM ME.

Frank took his phone from his pocket and called Bobby.

"Hello, Bobby," he said, "We've got a problem." Frank then relayed the message to Bobby, and the phone went very quiet at the other end.

"OK, Frank," said Bobby after a long pause, "get out of there and bring me the phone."

Frank and his colleague got back into their car, started the engine and pulled away sharply. They didn't notice the man sitting in a car about five spaces ahead of them. As they passed him, he raised his phone "They've just left Jack," he said. "OK, follow them," came the reply.

"What's the problem?" James asked.

"Give me one minute," Bobby replied. He walked across the reception and out of the door. When he got outside, he dialled a number on his phone.

"Hello Mum, it's Bobby," he said, "I know it's late, but I need you to do something for me."

"What?" she asked.

"I need you to put some things together," he told her, "you're going away for a few days."

"Why?" she pleaded, "where am I going?"

"Mum, please just do as I ask, I'll explain everything tomorrow," Bobby then called his men stationed outside his mum's house and explained exactly what he wanted them to do. He walked back into the hospital reception, where James sat looking very concerned.

"Bobby, what's going on?"

"James, this friend of yours, Lisa, tell me all about her," Bobby said.

"Well, we've lived together for a couple of years," he told him, "but only as friends," he added. "We've got a bit closer lately, but it's still at the very earliest stages," he said, "Why are you asking?"

"We've got a bit of a situation on our hands," said Bobby.

"What?" asked James looking quite frantic now.

"The Maclarens have got her," Bobby told him, deadpan.

"Who, Lisa?" he asked.

"Yes, I'm afraid so," he answered, "a couple of my blokes went to your house, and there was a note and a mobile phone and instructions to call them," he explained.

"Shit," exclaimed James, "what the fuck do we do now?"

"I'm not sure James, I'm really not sure," Bobby said with a hint of resignation in his voice.

"How much does she know?" Bobby asked.

"Nothing, she just thinks I've won the lottery," he replied. "If they hurt her, I swear I'll kill them myself."

"Calm down, James," his big brother told him, "there must be a way around this, let me think."

As they sat in silence, the entrance door opened, and Gary and Razor walked in.

"All right, guys?" Gary asked as he walked towards them. "No, it's not fucking all right!" James snapped at him, "The fucking Maclarens have kidnapped Lisa."

"James, keep your voice down," Bobby said, looking at him sternly.

Razor walked over to Bobby.

"What's going on, mate?"

Bobby updated him on the latest events.

"We need to get out of here," Bobby said, "come on James we're leaving."

James said goodbye to Gary and followed Razor and his brother out to the car. They drove in silence for a while until James could stand it no longer.

"What the fuck are we going to do?" he asked.

"I'm trying to figure it out," Bobby said.

As he spoke, his phone started to ring.

"Bobby, it's Frank, we're being followed," he said.

"Shit, where are you?" Bobby asked.

"We're coming through Streatham, on the way over to you," Frank told him.

Bobby's brain was working overtime.

"OK, do you know the cul-de-sac where Welsh Brian used to live?" he asked him.

"Yes," Frank replied.

"OK, lead him down there," he said, "we'll be waiting for you."

The road in question led to a scrapyard which belonged to a one-time friend, now enemy, of Bobby's. It was a very quiet road with only four houses in it located at the top of the road. The far end of the road was virtually deserted and perfect for what Bobby had in mind.

Ten minutes later, they were in place at the top of the road waiting for Frank.

"Here he comes," said Razor as a dark coloured Audi approached indicating to turn into the dead-end road.

As the Audi turned in another car followed, slowing as it got to the road. The driver seemed to be trying to see where his prey had gone.

"Go on, follow him!" Bobby urged.

The driver of the other car suddenly indicated and turned right following the Audi. Razor pulled forward so they could see down the road. He watched intently as the car passed the houses at the top of the road and continued further down. Bobby picked up his phone.

"Frank, stop there," he said. "Let's go Razor, we've got the bastard."

The black Range Rover pulled quickly into the dead end road and sped down to the other car which was now stationary. As they stopped Razor pulled the Range Rover across the road directly behind the following car making any attempt at escape impossible.

Bobby and Razor jumped out of the car and raced up to the driver's door. As Razor pulled the door open, they were joined by Frank, who was carrying a baseball bat. Bobby pulled the man from the car and threw him onto the bonnet. Laying on his back, the man looked terrified as Razor delivered a punch to the body, which forced him to curl into a ball. Bobby gave a nod to Frank, and he started to hit him around the legs with the bat. After about four blows, Bobby raised his hand to stop him.

"OK, cunt, where's the girl?" Bobby screamed at him. The man remained silent. Bobby nodded at Frank, who started raining more blows down. The man looked at Bobby, begging for mercy.

"Are you ready to answer my question now?" Bobby shouted at him again.

"I don't know," he said, almost crying, "please, believe me, I really don't know."

"Frank, open the boot of your car," Bobby instructed. Frank did as he was told whilst Razor pulled the man off the bonnet and dragged him towards Frank's car.

"Put him in there," Bobby ordered, and Razor duly obeyed. Frank slammed the boot shut with the man still pleading his innocence.

"OK, we'll take him over to the office block on Mears Road," said Bobby.

The men returned to their respective cars and headed for Mears Road. The building in question was being guarded by Bobby's security firm and was awaiting a complete internal refurbishment. When they arrived, they pulled up at the front gates of the site and were approached by a uniformed security guard. Bobby put the window down, and the security guard peered in.

"Good evening Mr Bolton," he said.

"Hello, Paul," Bobby replied, "open up, please."

"No problem."

He walked over to the gates and removed the chain, bonding them together. He eased the gates open. As they drove in, Bobby told Razor to stop, and he beckoned the guard over to the still open window.

"Just so we're clear, you haven't seen us tonight Paul," Bobby said. As he did, he passed the security guard a crisp new £50 note. The guard looked at the note and smiled.

"Never saw a thing, Mr Bolton."

"Good man," said Bobby reciprocating the guard's smile.

***

When Lisa awoke, she had no idea where she was or how she had got there. She was lying on an old Chesterfield sofa in what looked like a portacabin. Her hands and feet were bound. She managed to sit up and get a better look around. How on earth did she get here and why was she tied up? She could smell remnants of what smelled like chloroform. The smell started to slowly bring things back to her. There were men in her house, and they were looking for James, but she really couldn't remember any more than that.

"Help me!" she shouted but heard nothing in response. She struggled to her feet and hopped across the room to the window. That short distance strained every sinew of her body. It was a scrapyard. She couldn't see a soul, and the gates appeared to be locked. She shouted again but to no avail.

Suddenly she could hear dogs barking somewhere nearby. She looked from side to side and then saw the two Doberman's appear around the corner of the portacabin. They came to the window and looked up at her in silence. One of them went towards the door and started scratching at it keenly.

Chapter 15

Back at the Mears Road building, Bobby walked straight to the lift with Razor whilst Frank dragged their guest along behind them.

"Come on, James," Bobby shouted, "do you want to find your bird or not?"

James hurried along at the back of the group and was the last to enter the large freight lift. Razor pressed the button, and the lift made a steady rise until it reached the fourteenth floor. As the lift door groaned opened, Frank threw the man out of the door and onto the bare concrete floor. As James exited the lift, he immediately felt the pervading cold. He looked around and realised there was no glass in any of the windows.

"Get up," Bobby shouted at their captive. The man gingerly got to his feet and stood uneasily in front of Bobby. "Who are you?" Bobby demanded, eyes bulging.

Their captive just stared blankly back at him. "Who the fuck are you?" Bobby shouted even louder, "what's your name?" but still the man remained silent.

Razor stepped forward and hit the man full on the jaw, and he collapsed to the floor.

"Now hopefully that will have helped your memory," he said, "who are you and what are you doing following my boys around?"

"I'm nobody, and I know nothing," the man said through a grimace.

"Really!" Bobby laughed, "you are going to tell me where the girl is, or I'm gonna kill you, got it?"

"I don't know about any girl," he pleaded.

"Frank, pick him up!" Bobby ordered. Frank lifted the man from the floor and followed Bobby over to the open windows.

"Throw him out," said Bobby.

"What?" the man screamed in utter terror.

"I just told him to throw you out of the fucking window," Bobby told the petrified man, "if you ain't gonna tell me what I want to know then you're no fucking use to me," he continued. "Frank, do as you're told and throw him out of the fucking window!"

Frank and Razor lifted him and started to put him headfirst through the opened window. The man screamed, but they continued to lower him until he was hanging by his ankles.

"This is your last chance," Bobby said, but all the man could do was scream. Suddenly it went quiet.

"Fuck me, I think he's passed out!" laughed Razor.

"Cunt," Bobby said, laughing, "drag him back in."

They slowly, but methodically, pulled him back in through the window and threw him onto the floor. Bobby got his phone out and pointed it at the man on the floor.

"Straighten him up," Bobby said to Frank. Once he was laid out straight, Bobby took a head and shoulders photo of him.

"I'll send this photo to your boys. I want you to find out who he is?" Bobby instructed them. "Send the photo on to a few South London faces, someone will know him." The photo was sent to Razor and Frank, and they duly sent it on to friends and acquaintances.

"Frank give me the phone that was at the girl's house," Bobby said. Frank removed it from his jacket pocket and passed it to him.

"It's gone midnight, I hope I don't wake him," Bobby laughed.

He pressed the speed dial number as instructed and waited.

After four rings, it was answered.

"Hello," a voice said.

"Is that Billy Maclaren?" Bobby asked.

"It could be, who's this?" Billy asked.

"Don't worry about who I am you fucking mug! Deliver that girl home in the next hour, or I'm going to hunt you and your brother down and kill the fucking pair of you, got it?"

"I ain't doing a thing until I get my money," Billy replied calmly.

"Go fuck yourself," Bobby said, "you Maclaren boys can't afford to lose £850?" he laughed, "I thought you were supposed to be big-time?"

"It's the lottery ticket I want," Billy said.

"Listen, you scum," Bobby said, "I want to see that girl home safe before I even talk to you again, scummy cunt."

"Whoever you are, you owe me £72,000,000, and you will never see that girl until I get it," Billy screamed down the phone.

Bobby laughed, "Get it right, you prick," he said, "it was over £74,000,000 in fact, and you haven't got the ticket. You've got to be in it to win it, as they say, Billy," he goaded.

"I don't know who the fuck you are," Billy said, "but when I find out, I'm having my money and your bollocks you cunt."

"Just get that fucking girl home before you find out who I am and start regretting it!" Bobby hung up the phone abruptly.

During this verbal joust, the prostrate man had gradually come around, and Frank had tied his hands and feet.

"Are you going to talk to me or not?" Bobby said, looking down at the man. He didn't make any attempt to reply.

Bobby turned to walk away, and with the grace of an ice skater, he spun around swiftly and kicked the man straight in the face. He screamed out in agony as the blood poured from his nose and mouth.

"Frank, you and your bloke, stay here with him," Bobby said, "I'll send a couple of blokes over soon so you can get home for a kip. I'll need you both fresh tomorrow so don't lay in too late."

With that, Bobby walked towards the lift, followed by Razor and James. As the lift started on its way down, Bobby turned to James, "Are you OK, kid?" he asked him in a patronising tone.

"Yeah, I'm fine," James answered, "for a minute I thought they really had dropped him out of the window," he said.

Bobby laughed. "No point in killing him," he said, "I'm hoping to use him as a bargaining tool!"

"I am going out of my mind thinking about Lisa though," James said.

"I know son, but until we can find out where they're keeping her, there's not a lot we can do, unless you want to part with the money," Bobby told him.

They pulled away with Razor at the driver's wheel.

"Drop me and James at my mum's please," Bobby said.

"No problem," Razor replied.

"Oh, shit," said James, "I forgot about Mum, have you spoken to her?" he asked.

"Mum is fine and plotted up in a little boarding house in Brighton, all thanks to your generosity," Bobby told him.

"I'm very generous, aren't I?" They both laughed.

James had a sleepless night at his mum's house, worrying about Lisa. Bobby woke at about 7:00 am the next morning, and James made breakfast for them both. At exactly 7:30, there was a knock on the door, and Bobby answered. It was Razor.

They disappeared into the living room, and James could make them out speaking in whispers. Bobby came back into the kitchen.

"OK, let's sort out how we're going to get your girl back," he said, smiling, which James found reassuring. They went out to the car and drove off in the direction of Mears Road. As they drove, James was thinking about Lisa. How frightened she must be and how much she must hate him for getting her involved in this maelstrom.

"When you phone that Billy again, see if he'll let me talk to Lisa please," he asked his brother, "I want to know that she's OK."

"I'll see what I can do," Bobby grunted.

They pulled up to the site, and the guard smiled and opened the gate for them.

"Don't let anyone in without calling me first," Bobby said to the guard who nodded in agreement.

They entered the building and took the elevator up to the fourteenth floor where their guest was now seated on a chair, hands and legs still bound and looking a bit worse for wear.

Two of Bobby's guys had been there babysitting all night and looked weary. "Go and get some coffee and bring it back and whilst you're out, phone Frank and tell him to come back." The two men headed for the lift and once inside the doors slammed behind them.

"Well, how are we doing this morning?" Bobby asked their prisoner.

"Fuck off!" he yelled.

"My, but we are brave this morning," Bobby laughed. "Now do we feel in the mood for answering some of my questions today, Peter?" The man's head spun around quickly towards Bobby as he realised, they knew who he was. Bobby and Razor started to laugh as James looked on puzzled.

"How rude of me, I forgot to introduce you," Bobby said, looking at James. "James, meet Pete Maclaren, Billy's brother."

***

101

As Billy arrived at the yard just after seven in the morning, the gate was already open, and the dogs were sleeping in the kennel. He walked up the stairs to the top cabin and went in. Jack was sitting at his desk, drinking coffee and talking on the phone.

"I don't know Mum," he said, "I asked him to do a little job for me yesterday, and I haven't heard from him since. I gave him a few quid before he left so he's probably been on the piss," he added. "He'll turn up soon, I'll call you later." He hung up the phone.

"What's going on?" Billy asked.

"Pete went to keep an eye on that bird's house yesterday," he told him, "he phoned to say that some blokes had been round there and I told him to follow them, but I've heard nothing since."

"I don't know why the fuck you send him out on these jobs," Billy said angrily.

"He'll be all right," Jack said.

"Where's the girl?" Billy asked.

"I put her in the other office out the back," he said, "she'll be all right there."

"Did you rough her up?" Billy asked.

"No, but I had a little feel of her tits as I pushed her into the office," Jack said, laughing.

"You're a fucking animal, Jack," Billy said, shaking his head. "Anyway, I want you to get on the phone and get some of the boys together. I don't know who this geezer is, but I think this whole thing could get very nasty."

Jack nodded his consent and started scrolling through his phone. Pretty soon he had a small army ready to report for action as and when called upon.

Billy left the office and walked around to the second office where the girl was being kept. He unlocked the door and walked in to see her seated on the floor hands and feet still bound.

"Morning," he said. Lisa turned her head and refused to answer. "I hope you've changed your attitude after a night in here?"

"Why don't you fuck off!" Lisa spat the words out.

"Where is your boyfriend?" he asked. Lisa remained silent. "OK, another question," Billy said, "who does he know that would want to start threatening me?"

Lisa wondered what he could mean but remained silent, much to the annoyance of Billy. Lisa looked directly at him. "What is it that James has done to piss you off?" she asked. "Surely you know?" he said, "he owes me over £70,000,000 quid."

"How does he owe you that?" Lisa asked.

"He stole my lottery ticket," Billy told her.

"Oh, for fuck's sake," she exclaimed.

"I will ask you once again," Billy said, "where is he?"

"£70,000,000 buys a lot of hiding places," she laughed, "if it were me, I'd be well gone by now."

"That's the strange thing," said Billy, "he hasn't made a run for it, he actually seems more worried about finding you."

"Really?" she said, surprised.

"I'm starting to get a bit pissed off with this," he said, "I may have to send my nutty brother in to speak to you, and I really don't think you'll enjoy that."

"Fuck him," she said.

"I think you'll find that's his plan for you," Billy laughed as he walked out and locked the door behind him.

Billy walked back into the main office to see Jack had been joined by a few of his heavies. They were all sprawled on the sofa and over his desk.

"Come on you lot," he said, "out of here I've got work to do." They all started to parade out, Billy opened the drawer in his desk and pulled out £50.

"Here you are guys, go and have breakfast on me," he said as he passed the money over to the last guy in the queue to leave. As they left, Billy heard a phone ringing, he knew it was them. He answered.

"Changed your mind yet?" Billy said as he answered the phone.

"Not in the slightest but I have noticed that you haven't delivered the girl back yet," Bobby replied.

"I hadn't noticed you dropping off that seventy-odd million he owes me either," Billy said, "now let me tell you, this girl will start to suffer if this is not sorted out pretty soon," he told him.

"That reminds me," said Bobby, "This hostage game is fun, isn't it?" he continued, "I've got one as well now."

"What the fuck are you talking about?" Billy asked. "Well, whatever you may do to that girl we're going to do to our hostage," Bobby told him.

"You're full of shit," Billy said.

"Really?" Bobby replied, "Have you spoken to your brother Pete lately?"

"What?" Billy asked.

"You shouldn't send your nearest and dearest to follow my guys," he said, "especially when they're as fucking stupid as this cunt."

"You lay a finger on my brother, and I'll fucking kill you and all your family," Billy shouted.

"Do you know we dangled him out of the window by his ankles last night and the prick fainted, he's got no bollocks just like you and Jack," Bobby laughed.

"When I find out who you are, you're dead," Billy said with pure venom in his voice.

"Yeah, I think you mentioned that yesterday," Bobby reminded him, "now just let the girl go, and you can have your pathetic excuse of a brother back."

"What about my money?" Billy asked.

"Go fuck yourself," Bobby said, "I'll call you later and tell you where to drop her off and don't fuck me about, or your brother will go out of the window. That's a promise." Bobby hung up the phone.

"Did he go for it?" James asked.

"We'll see later," Bobby answered. "If this works and we get Lisa back he'll still want his money, you know that don't you?" said Bobby.

"Well I kind of guessed that," answered James.

"He's not fucking having it," said Bobby defiantly, "but there will be a war because he will never stop looking for you."

"I kind of guessed that too," said James.

"What do you want to do?" Bobby asked, "run with the money and spend the rest of your life looking over your shoulder or stay and fight and hopefully teach him such a lesson that he will never want to come anywhere near our family again."

"You've probably saved Lisa's life," James said to his brother, "I'm with you till the end," he promised.

Chapter 16

"That cunt's got Pete," Billy said to Jack, "Why the fuck did you send him out to follow them?" he asked.

"Well, he can't do anything else!" Jack replied.

"Yeah, and now we know he can't do that either," Billy shouted at his older brother, "we're fucked now, we'll have to let the girl go, and that was our only way of keeping in touch," said Billy, getting increasingly irate. "This is all your fucking fault, Jack!"

"Can I go and fuck her before we let her go?" Jack said, a sinister grin spreading across his craggy features.

"You'd probably do that wrong as well," Billy said.

"So what do we do now?" Jack snapped.

"We've got no choice, we've got to let her go," Billy replied. "We don't know who this bloke is, but he's threatening to throw Pete out of a window."

"I'll fucking kill him," Jack said.

"Kill who?" Billy asked.

"Whoever this fucking bloke is."

"Exactly," Billy said, "we don't even know who the fuck he is, we need to let the girl go and concentrate on finding who this prick is and take it from there."

Billy sat very quietly ruminating on the situation he found himself in.

***

"Right then," said Bobby, "we need to have a plan as to how to collect Lisa."

"Obviously, it needs to be somewhere public," Razor offered.

"Yeah, who does she know that we can trust to go and meet her?" Bobby asked James.

"Why can't I go?" said James.

"I think that's too dangerous," Bobby replied, "me and Razor can't go either," he continued, "as it stands, they don't know who we are and I'd like it to stay that way."

"We could send Gary?" James suggested.

"Does she know him?" Razor asked.

"Not too well, but she knows he's a mate of mine," James told them.

"OK, let's go to the hospital and pick him up."

The three of them got into Bobby's car and headed for the private hospital. Whilst driving, Bobby was formulating a plan in his head.

"I think you should go away for a couple of days, James," he told him.

"Really, I thought you wanted me to stay?"

"I do, but I think if you're out of the way for a few days they are more likely to slip up whilst looking for you."

"OK," said James, "but what about Lisa?" he asked.

"Take her with you, if she's still talking to you," he answered, laughing.

Whilst travelling, Bobby made a few calls and arranged for a new car to be delivered to them for James to use. They then turned to the small matter of assembling a small army for the oncoming conflict.

They arrived at the hospital and saw the car outside with Bobby's guy's keeping a lookout.

When they entered the hospital, James headed immediately for Terry's room whilst Razor, and Bobby held back talking.

"Tell Gary I want a word," he called to James.

"Will do."

Terry was still in a bad way. He had come out of his coma the day before but was still sleeping a lot. His memory of what happened to him was still very limited. James entered the room and saw Gary half asleep in the armchair.

"Good bodyguard, you are!" he said, smiling.

"Hello mate," Gary replied, "where have you been, I haven't seen you in ages?"

"Trying to sort all this mess out," he told him. "Anyway, my brother wants a word with you."

"And that's another thing," Gary said, "you never told me that Bobby Bolton was your brother."

"Well, I never really knew quite what he was involved in," James told him.

"He's a fucking legend North of the river," Gary said.

"So, I'm starting to understand," replied James, "anyway he's got a job for you."

"Oh fuck," said Gary leaving the room.

James approached the bed where his best mate lay. He looked awful. James didn't really know what to say to him.

"Hello, Terry," he said. Terry turned his head to look at him.

"You finally turned up then," he whispered.

"I'm sorry mate," James replied, "there's a lot of shit to sort out."

"You're telling me," Terry exclaimed, "look at the fucking state of me, whatever you did they think I'm involved, and you fucked off and left me to take the kicking."

"I'm sorry Terry, I didn't know what was going on either."

"Gary said you won the lottery?"

"Yeah, I did, that's the problem," James told him.

"How the fuck is that a problem?" Terry asked.

"It transpired it was Billy Maclaren's ticket," James informed him. "How's my luck?"

"What, you stole his lottery ticket, and it won?" he asked.

"I didn't steal it," James said, "I found it."

"Well I hope you've given it back," Terry said.

"Nope, I've cashed it in of course. I didn't know it was McLaren's at the time."

"You must be fucking mad," Terry told him, "how much was it for?" he asked.

"£74 million quid," James answered.

Terry started to laugh, but it was obviously causing him pain. "My best mate becomes a multimillionaire, and all I get is a stay in a private hospital, Cheers pal."

"When all this is over, I promise I will look after you," said James.

"Really?" replied Terry, "what's the going rate for four busted ribs, a broken ankle and six days in a coma?" he asked. "I'm not sure," replied James, "perhaps we can negotiate," he said, breaking into a laugh.

Terry looked back at him and started to smile "You bastard!"

The door opened, and Bobby walked in.

"How's the patient?"

"Getting better," James informed him.

"Terry," James said, "meet my brother Bobby, he's going to sort all this out."

"So I've heard," Terry said, "I hope you know what you're dealing with?"

"I think so," Bobby said smiling, "Gary won't be around for the next day, or so, I've got a couple of things I want him to do for me," he told Terry, "but I've got two blokes outside in case Maclarens lot turn up here."

"Thanks a million," Terry answered sarcastically.

"You're welcome," Bobby said, smiling.

Bobby and James said their goodbyes and left Terry alone in his room. As they entered the hospital reception, they saw Razor talking to a man who James had not seen before.

"Hi, Bobby," the man said, "here are the keys."

"Thanks," Bobby said, handing the keys to James.

"You've just bought yourself a new car," he told him. They left the hospital and Razor escorted James over to a brand-new Mercedes AMG.

"Don't put your foot down too hard," Razor told him, "cars like this take a bit of getting used to."

Bobby got in the car with James and had a look around. "Nice motor," he said.

"Yeah, not bad," replied James. "How much did I spend on this?" he asked.

"Not exactly sure," Bobby replied, "but whatever it is you can afford it."

***

Billy and Jack were sitting in the office when the phone rang.

"Hello," Billy said.

"Listen to me," Bobby said, "drop the girl outside Stockwell Tube Station in one hour," he ordered. "Someone will walk her away, and when they are both at a safe distance, I will send your brother to the same spot, got that?"

"When do I get to meet you, then?" Billy inquired.

"Don't worry about that, you'll meet me soon enough, you just won't know when, until it's too late."

"Fuck you!" Billy said.

Bobby started to laugh down the phone, "One hour," he said.

"We've got to drop her in Stockwell," Billy told his brother, "I want at least twenty blokes around watching everything," he ordered. "I want to know who this scumbag is."

Billy went to the back office and unlocked the door. Lisa was sitting on the floor, still shackled.

"Oh, what a privilege," she said, "visitors."

"Fuck you, you little bitch," Billy said, "I want to know who this cunt is who's helping your boyfriend?"

"I told you I don't know, and he's 'NOT' my boyfriend." Billy started to untie her feet. When he had finished, he pulled her up and pushed her towards the door. She squinted as she hit the full force of the sunlight.

"Where are we going?" she asked. Billy did not reply. Jack came out of the other office.

"I've got everyone I can, and I've sent them to get in position," he told Billy.

"Right get her in the car and take one of the young boys with you, I'll follow in my car," he instructed him. "When you get there, stop on the corner and let the boy walk her over to the front of the station and leave her there."

"OK Bill," he said.

Jack pulled Lisa over to a two-door BMW and after lowering the front seat pushed her into the rear of the car. The boy sat in the front with Jack. They drove in silence. Lisa was looking out of the side window, trying to work out where they were heading. Suddenly she recognised that they were passing through Brixton and then on towards Stockwell. As they approached the station, Jack started to slow down and eventually came to a stop on the corner of the council estate that ran adjacent to the underground station.

As they stopped, the boy got out of the vehicle and leaned into the back to untie Lisa's hands. Once untied, he pulled her forward out of the vehicle.

"When you get to the station, leave her and come back to the car," he told the boy. "Don't you try to run," he said to Lisa, "our people are very close."

As they walked across to the station entrance the boy held her by the arm, once there he let go of her and walked away. Lisa stood alone for a few seconds and suddenly saw Gary approaching her.

"Straight into the station," he told her, taking her by the arm and down the stairs. As they reached the bottom of the stairs, Lisa suddenly heard three large explosions and the station began to fill with smoke.

Pandemonium broke out as everyone was rushing to leave the station by the main exit. Gary held Lisa's arm and rushed towards the escalator. Quickly touching two tickets onto the barrier, they rushed through and onto the moving escalator. As Lisa looked back, all she could see was smoke and people running for the exits.

"It's OK," Gary assured her, "we're perfectly safe, just keep moving." As they got to the platform, the train was just pulling in, and they jumped straight on it.

"Gary, what is going on?" Lisa asked as the train pulled away from the platform.

"Just a few bangers and a smoke bomb," he answered, "diversionary tactics," he said, smiling.

As the smoke cleared back at Stockwell Station, the only people still inside were Billy and four of his men. As he looked around, he saw his very dazed brother sitting on the ground, leaning against the ticket machine.

"Fuck it," he said, very loudly.

Gary and Lisa travelled one station to the Oval where they got off. They went up the escalator to the main concourse, touched their tickets at the barrier and walked out of the station. Sitting outside was a brand-new Mercedes. Gary opened the front door and ushered Lisa inside. As soon as the door was closed, the car pulled away.

"How you doing?" a voice asked.

She turned her head to see James at the steering wheel.

"You total wanker," she said.

"If I said I'm sorry, would it help?" he asked.

"Probably not," she replied, "a full explanation wouldn't go amiss though."

James phone started to ring, he pressed the button on the steering wheel, and Bobby's voice filled the car.

"Hi Lisa, I'm Bobby, James's brother."

"Brother," said Lisa, "what brother?" she said, looking at James.

"I'll explain later," he said.

"Everything went to plan then," Bobby asked.

"Like clockwork," he replied.

"Good, Razor has just picked Gary up," he informed them, "we're going to lay low for a few days and see what they do next so have a nice time and keep in touch," Bobby said, as he hung up the phone.

"You haven't even asked how I am," Lisa said, "and where did this brother come from, where are we going and what the fuck has been happening?"

"First things first," he said, "where do you want to go?"

"Home," she replied.

"Ah, that's one place I can't take you," he told her. "It's too dangerous by far."

"I can't go home! You're kidding!" she asked.

"No, I'm afraid not."

"James, I've been kidnapped, threatened and kept in a filthy container for the last few days. I would like a drink, a bath, a change of clothes and I would still like a fucking good explanation," she said, "but not necessarily in that order," she added showing she still retained a modicum of humour.

"OK," said James, "let's head up towards the Cotswolds, we can stop on the way to get you a change of clothes, book into a hotel and you can spend as long as you like in the bath."

"And on the way there I want a bloody explanation," she added.

"You'll get one."

***

Billy Maclaren was furious. "How the fuck did they get away?" he kept asking. Jack kept his head down, and most of the others had disappeared.

"So, what can you tell us?" Billy said, turning to his other brother Pete.

"Nothing really," he said, "I didn't recognise any of them."

"They must have called each other by name," Billy said.

"I think one of them was called Razor," Pete said.

"I hope that's not Razor Richards out of Tottenham," one of the boys said.

"Why?" asked Jack, "Who's he then?"

"You must know him," the man said, "he's one of the meanest bastards in the whole of London."

"Well, who does he work with?" asked Billy.

"Bobby Bolton," the man replied.

"Of course!" said Billy, "this James must be related to Bobby Bolton, how did I not make that connection?" he added. "Right then Jack, if this firm is as good as their reputation, we're going to need a few more blokes, may even have to bring some in from outside of London."

"Are we going to war with them?" Jack asked.

"Fucking right we are," said Billy, "we've got 74,000,000 reasons to kill these bastards, and that's what we're going to do."

Bobby's phone rang as he and Razor were driving home.

"Hello," he said and then listened for about twenty seconds. He hung up the phone laughing.

"That was Jack," he said, "they've found out who we are and there still looking for a war." They were both laughing now.

Bobby dialled a number on his phone.

"Hello Kenny, its Bobby," he said, "they know it's me now, are you ready to go to war?" he asked.

"Most definitely," he said, "I'll start rounding the troops up, I owe that bastard one."

"Cheers mate," Bobby hung up the phone.

Chapter 17

War

London is a very tribal city split into four major geographical areas: North, South, East and West. Each is ruled by their own local villains. These gangs would be made up of a small hardcore of villains who would be on the weekly payroll and generally be involved in drugs, debt collection or protection rackets. They would then have their foot soldiers who would be called up at very short notice to join them in some form of violent confrontation. Whether on the weekly payroll or just being bought in as and when required, these gang members were fiercely loyal. Very rarely does one step into another's 'manor' as it is called. What is even more rare is for gangs to cross the 'water' (River Thames) as it is known to face each other.

This was about to change.

South London had not seen a true gang war on this scale for years. This was likely to be the first since the late 1960s when the Richardson's ruled the roost. It was the main topic of conversation in the pubs and clubs frequented by the underworld community. On the Southside of the river people knew of Bobby by reputation only and, although the Maclarens where an out and out South London mob, they were not the most popular of people. Many South Londoners were in fact secretly hoping the Maclarens would get a bit of a hiding.

What puzzled most people was that although it was public knowledge about the fallout, nobody seemed to know exactly what had occurred to start the argument.

Phone calls were being made and allegiances being tested as the days went by. Bobby made sure he was surrounded by his best men as he waited for the Maclarens to make their opening move.

It wouldn't take long.

Billy was in his office at the yard. With him was Jack and eight of his most loyal and reliable soldiers.

"The way I see it," said Billy, "is that we should send a big message to this geezer by taking out his best man first," he continued, "I think we need to take this Razor bloke out of the game."

"How do you suggest we do that?" asked Jack.

"Dave," he said, looking over at one of his gang members, "do you fancy taking a couple of your boys and blowing this cunt away?" Billy asked. "It would really put in a marker that we mean business."

"No problem," he replied, "if you can get your guys to try and find out where he lives and hangs out, then I can do the rest."

"Good man," said Billy, "if we can shake him up by hitting his best mate, he's more likely to come out all guns blazing, and that will be his downfall," he added.

"Has anyone had any joy tracking down the little brother or the girl?" Jack asked. He looked around the room but was met with blank and silent faces.

"OK," said Billy, "I'm pissed off sitting around waiting; let's get things started."

It was a quiet evening in the Crown. The usual crowd that came in straight from work had started to get off home to their wives and kids, whilst a few of the un-married had decided to go to the local snooker hall for a few frames. This left about six people sitting in the bar with the jukebox quietly playing a piece of classical music from the random play repertoire. Geoff walked over to the small box on the wall behind the bar and pressed the reject button only for the classical music to be replaced with a nineteen seventies Bay City Rollers number. He had noticed a drop in his takings since the business with the Maclarens started, most people knew that the trouble had something to do with one of his regulars and were keeping well away. Although he had always had a reasonably good relationship with the Maclarens, he knew that would in no way stop them from trashing his pub, and he was right.

He had just finished serving one of his few customers and was walking out into the office to retrieve his cigarettes when he heard a car pull up outside. As he turned to see if anyone was coming in, he heard the sound of breaking glass and a bottle smashed through the window. The bottle was alight, and the smell of petrol filled the air as it ignited the carpet. Within seconds it was like an inferno, and the pub was filling with acrid smoke.

"Everyone this way," he shouted. Urging people to follow him behind the bar and towards the back door, as they started coming through, he heard another smash and saw a second bottle light up another part of the pub. He was dialling the emergency services as he left via the back door and saw a car speeding off down the road.

Geoff was sitting on the pavement, coughing up all the smoke that had got into his lungs when the fire brigade arrived and aimed their hoses into his pub. He sat and watched as his business literally went up in smoke. The only consolation was that they managed to extinguish the fire before it reached the upper levels, which contained all his personal belongings.

Most of the fire crew had gone inside the pub to make sure everything was out and left one officer checking the exterior.

"Excuse me, mate?" the fireman called.

"What's up?" asked Geoff.

"Does this mean anything to you?" he said, pointing at the wall.

Geoff stood up and walked over to where the firefighter was pointing, he looked at the wall of the pub and saw scrawled:

I want my fucking money back

Geoff took his phone from his pocket and scrolled through until he came to James, he pressed the dialled number. *I'm sorry this number is no longer in use*, a voice informed him. *Shit,* thought Geoff. Scrolling through again, he found Gary's number.

"Hello Gary, it's Geoff."

"Hi mate," Gary replied, "everything OK," he asked.

"No, it's not fucking, OK," Geoff shouted down the phone "I've just had a visit from the Maclarens."

"Oh Shit," said Gary, "what did they say?"

"They didn't say a fucking word, they just petrol-bombed my pub and wrote a message on the wall stating they want their money back."

"OK Geoff, try and calm down and leave it with me," Gary said, "I'm sure James won't let you end up out of pocket."

"You tell him he best sort this mess out and fucking soon," Geoff said and hung up the phone abruptly.

Gary immediately called Bobby and told him what had occurred at the Crown and passed on Geoff's message.

"OK," Bobby said, "I'll talk to James."

James and Lisa were enjoying a meal at the beautiful Cotswold hotel they had booked in to, blissfully unaware of recent events in London. They had spent the day shopping in the local town and then wandering through the countryside discussing what their next step should be.

They had decided that Lisa would stay away from London until all of this was sorted out, but James felt he should go back and join his brother in the war against the Maclarens.

"But you're not that kind of man," she said to him. "You're way out of your depth!"

"I know," James replied, "but I caused all of this trouble, so the least I can do is be there when it all kicks off," he told her. "Are you sure they're not all doing this just to get a share of your money?" Lisa asked.

"I'm sure some of them are," he replied, "but Bobby isn't so I must be there with him."

Lisa didn't agree but didn't argue. As far as she was concerned if they were to become a couple which was looking more and more likely, they should just get as far away from all these people. Go somewhere where they wouldn't be found and live a life of luxury. James tried to explain to her that these people would never stop looking for him, and in the meantime, all of his friends and family were at risk.

James phone started to ring. He glanced down and saw it was his brother.

"Hi, Bobby," he said.

"James it's started," Bobby told him.

"What's started?" James asked.

"The war. The Maclarens have just firebombed, the boozer," he explained.

"What, The Crown?" he asked.

"That's the one," Bobby replied.

"Is everyone OK?" James enquired.

"Yes, the governor is a bit shaken up, but he'll survive," he told his brother.

"I'm coming back tomorrow," James said.

"OK, but find somewhere for Lisa to stay," he advised.

"I will, of course, I will."

The following morning James showered and shaved before escorting Lisa down to the restaurant for breakfast. They were seated at a table beside the open fire, which took the chill out of the air on a very cold November morning.

As they were waiting for their breakfast to be served, James noticed something different about Lisa.

"What's up with you this morning?" he asked.

"Lots of things," she said, "but mainly I'm worried about you going back to London."

"I'll be ok, don't worry," he informed her.

"But you don't know that," she said. "You could end up dead."

"Bobby will see that I'm all right," he said.

"Look James I don't want to seem like I'm putting a dampener on the big family reunion, but a few days ago you didn't even know if your brother was alive or dead and now, he's the messiah."

"Well he probably saved your life," James replied.

"I know," said Lisa, "and I'm not ungrateful, but I'm worried," she continued. "Could you not just do a deal with these people and give them some of the money back?" she asked.

"I think it's too late for that now," he said, "they firebombed the Crown last night."

Lisa just looked at him with a very frightened look on her face. The waitress approached the table and served them each with an enormous full English breakfast.

James thanked the waitress and started to pour the tea.

"So where am I dropping you off?" he asked her.

"I thought I might go and stay with an old school friend near Northampton if that's ok with you?" said Lisa.

"Not a problem," he replied, "just get me a postcode, and we can try and work out how the Sat Nav works on this new car."

"I've got her address in my purse," she said.

They finished their breakfast and went back to their suite. Whist Lisa sorted out her belongings and placed them into the new suitcase James called his brother to let him know his plans and what time to expect him.

"I'll text you an address to meet me at," Bobby told him "We need to keep away from your place and Mum's for the time being, they'll be watching both gaffs."

"OK," James said, "speak later."

James and Lisa pulled out of the hotel car park and set off towards the motorway following the Sat Nav system. They discussed many things on the way but left alone the difficult subject of their relationship. James was so keen to tell her how much he loved her and how he wanted to spend the rest of his life with her but felt that with all the other business going on it wasn't the right time. Lisa was having exactly the same feelings for him but was so afraid what may happen back in London that she dare not say anything.

When they reached their destination James parked outside, got out and opened the boot of the car. He retrieved Lisa's suitcase and followed her to the front door. She rang the bell and a few moments later, the door was opened by a petite blonde woman.

"Hey, Lisa!" she said with a huge smile on her face. The two women embraced as James stood behind Lisa feeling a bit embarrassed.

"So, who's this hunk?" the woman said to Lisa whilst looking at James.

"Oh, how rude of me," Lisa said, "Vanessa, this is James."

"Hi, James," Vanessa said.

"Hi," he replied.

James followed the two women into the house and put Lisa's suitcase in the hallway.

"Cup of tea James?" Vanessa called from the kitchen.

"No, thanks, I've got to get going," he replied.

Lisa turned to James "Really," she asked, "you don't have time for a cup of tea?"

"No, I'm sorry, I must go," he told her.

"Don't use your bank card while you're here," he said.

"What? Why not?" she said, looking very confused.

"They checked out my bank account, so they obviously have someone on the inside," he told her. "I've had to change my account to a more secure one due to the amount of money I have in there."

"So, what do I do if I need money?" she asked.

James put his hand into the inside pocket of his jacket and pulled out a bundle of £50 notes.

"There's £1,000 here to tide you over," he said, "if you need any more, just call me on my new number."

"Thank you," she said.

"And remember, don't give this number to anyone, not even your friend," he told her.

"I won't, I promise."

James went to give her a kiss goodbye and in return got the sweetest and most sensuous kiss he had ever received.

"Wow!" he said, "I'll be back for more of that."

Lisa smiled at him. "You make sure you are," she said, "and don't make it too long. Just be careful."

James turned and walked back down the path towards his car. Lisa stood at the door watching him leave, "I love you," she whispered very quietly.

James got into his car and started it. As he pulled away, he waved to Lisa, and she waved back.

He pressed a couple of buttons on his steering wheel and was through to Bobby.

"Hi," he said, "I'm just leaving Northampton. I'll be with you in about two hours."

"Did you get the address I sent you?" Bobby asked.

"Yes," replied James, "I'll see you there."

Chapter 18

"Hello," Bobby said as he answered his phone.

"Bobby it's Frank," the voice the other end said.

"Where are you?"

"We're outside the house, he's just gone in," Frank told him "What do you want us to do next," he asked.

"It's up to you, Frank," Bobby said, "you can go in and do him in his house if you want."

"I don't think so," Frank replied, "he's got a couple of young kids in there."

"In that case, wait for him to leave and follow him," Bobby said, "Wait till you get to somewhere suitable and do him there, OK?"

"No problem, Bobby."

Frank and his companion were sitting in a car across the road from the house of a man named Chris Davies. He was one of the Maclarens top men and had been involved in the underworld all his life. Chris was a habitual criminal and like many had done his fair share of time inside prison where he built up quite a reputation of being a hard and ruthless bastard. After his last stint inside he had decided to retire from the frontline of crime and got more involved in the running of the Maclaren business along with Billy. They had been friends since they were kids and Billy trusted Chris with his life. Billy had been best man at his wedding a couple of years previously when the mother of his three young children eventually agreed to marry him. Tonight, he was Bobby's first target.

Frank had waited for nearly two hours when, eventually, there was some movement. A car pulled up outside the target's house, and a man got out and walked briskly to the front door. He knocked on the door, and Chris opened it.

"I'll be two minutes," they heard Chris tell the man, who after acknowledging him returned to his car.

"That must be a minicab," Frank said to his colleague, "try not to hurt him, wouldn't be fair, would it?"

After a couple of minutes, Chris appeared at the door again as he walked through the door, a blonde woman appeared behind him. He turned back and gave her a kiss. "I won't be late," Frank heard him say. Chris followed the garden path and got into the minicab.

As it pulled away, Frank was watching in his mirrors. A car came along the road, and Frank pulled out behind it. They could see Chris' minicab one car ahead of them and followed for about a mile before it took a left turn and Frank followed. They seemed to be heading towards the docks, and Frank really didn't want to get caught down there, being a North London boy, he didn't know Docklands too well and could easily get lost. The car took a right turn, and once into the road, it slowed down as if looking for an address. Ahead Frank could see a building which was lit up, and he could hear music coming from the house. The minicab pulled up just before the lit building double parking on the street. Frank pulled alongside with his window down he looked across to the passenger side of the minicab.

"Oi, Chris!" he shouted. The man in the other car turned with a smile, obviously thinking it must be a friend. His face changed as he looked into Frank's eyes.

"Got a message for your guv'nor," Frank exclaimed with a sufficient air of menace. At that moment Frank produced a 38mm revolver and pointed it at Chris. Before he could move, Frank had let off three rounds right into the face of Billy Maclaren's best mate. The sound of gunfire erupted into the night air, and people came rushing out of the party and towards the two cars. Frank put his arm out of the window and pointing the gun directly into the air he let of two more rounds which stopped everybody in their tracks.

"Tell Billy Maclaren he's fucking with the wrong people this time!" he shouted towards the crowd gathered there and managed to wheelspin the BMW as he sped off.

Frank was straight on the phone to Bobby.

"It's done," he told him.

"Topman Frank," Bobby replied, "you know where to go now don't you?"

"Yeah, I'm on my way," Frank replied and hung up the phone abruptly.

Frank got back to the main road and slowed down so as not to draw attention to themselves. As they drove an ambulance with sirens and flashing lights came past them travelling towards the carnage they had just caused.

They drove for about another ten minutes until they arrived at an old derelict block of garages that Bobby had told him to make for. As they pulled in, Frank saw one of Bobby's guys standing alone at the opposite end. He pulled up next to him.

"Jump out quick," the man said.

As Frank and his partner leapt from the car, the other man started pouring petrol onto the back seat and then the front. Just as Frank turned the corner, he saw the man throw a lit cloth into the back, and the whole thing went up in flames. The other man ran to join them and pushed them in the direction of a dark grey Audi that was waiting there for them. Once in the Audi, they sped off into the night.

Billy was sitting at home, watching TV with his wife when he got the call. "Hello," he said.

"Billy, it's Jack."

"What's up?" Billy asked.

"You better brace yourself," Jack said, and then told him what had happened earlier in the evening.

As Billy disconnected the call, he was already up the stairs and in his bedroom pulling clothes out of his wardrobe. He dressed in seconds and was running down the stairs.

"What's happened?" his wife called as she followed him around the house.

"It's Chris," he shouted back to her, "those bastards have shot him in the face."

He ran through the kitchen and out into the garage where he unlocked a steel cabinet which appeared empty. He then produced another key and placed it into a lock at the rear of the cabinet and a panel came loose. He reached inside and retrieved a handgun, a trusted weapon he had deployed many times previously. Putting it into his pocket he raced back through the kitchen and out of the front door to where a car, sent by Jack, was already waiting for him he jumped in, and they moved off at high speed.

***

DI John Hobbs was the first detective on-site at the shooting. There were a lot of people hanging around trying to see what was happening. He showed his identification to a uniformed officer who let him through the cordon.

"Who was first here?" he asked another uniformed officer who was standing near the minicab.

"PC Fuller – he's over there talking to the paramedic," he replied, pointing.

Hobbs approached the ambulance and made himself known to both men.

"What's the state of play?" he asked.

"It appears that a car pulled up alongside this minicab and the driver called to the passenger. As the passenger turned, he let rip with a revolver," PC Fuller.

"What's the condition of the victim?" Hobbs asked the paramedic.

"He was still alive when they left here for the hospital, but I wouldn't expect him to last too long," he replied. "There was extensive bleeding from the face and neck. Not pretty."

"Do we know who he is?" Hobbs enquired.

PC Fuller opened his notebook and started reading. "According to his driving licence, it's Christopher Davies," he said.

"As in Billy Maclaren's right-hand man, that Chris Davies?"

"I'm not sure," the PC replied, "his face was not recognisable, but he was about the right size," he told him "and I've heard whispers of revenge since I've been here."

"Shit," said Hobbs, "just what we need, a fucking gang war."

He looked around the scene, slowly shaking his head.

"Did anyone see the shooter?" Hobbs asked.

"Only as he was driving away," Fuller told him. "He apparently shot twice in the air and shouted something about Billy Maclaren and drove off."

"Shit! This is going to escalate, no doubt about it." Fuller took Hobbs to speak to the mini-cab driver who was sitting in the back of the ambulance. He had a blanket around his shoulders, partly due to the cold but also to cover his clothes which were splattered with the blood of the victim.

Hobbs spoke to him for a few minutes and then decided there was no more he could do at the crime scene and went back to his car to return to the station. As he drove, he called his sergeant.

"Colin, John Hobbs here," he said, "we've got a problem, a big problem."

"Another one, sir?" Sgt Colin Murray replied.

"Billy Maclaren's mate Chris Davies has been shot, and it looks like we've got a war starting," Hobbs told him. "I want you over to St. George's hospital and watch who goes in and out."

"OK, Guv, I'm on my way," he replied.

"Whilst you're there get on the phone to anyone who may have some information about how this started," Hobbs added. "Will do," Murray said as Hobbs hung up.

Hobbs arrived at the station and went straight to the canteen which was now closed. He checked his pockets for some change and headed for the vending machine. With a plastic cup of lukewarm, insipid coffee, he wandered along the corridor to his office. After removing his overcoat and jacket, he sat at the desk and turned his computer on. He typed in the name Christopher Davies and pressed enter. After a few seconds, the screen became filled with a complete biography of Davies' criminal career, known associates and any potential enemies. He then searched the name Billy Maclaren to see if there were any enemies in common. Only one showed up, and after another search, Hobbs discovered that this individual was three years into a ten stretch at Woodhill Prison.

Hobbs leaned back in his chair and drained his coffee cup as the phone on his desk rang. He picked up the receiver.

"Hobbs," he said.

"Hello, Guv, Colin here," Sgt. Murray said.

"Anything happening over there?" Hobbs enquired.

"Both the Maclarens have been in, and a couple of their boys," Murray told him, "They were both surrounded by heavies as though they were being protected."

"Sounds like they're expecting something serious," Hobbs said. "There must be some really heavy shit going down, we need to find out what's going on."

"All I've been able to find out is that there's a lot of money involved," Murray informed him.

"OK," Hobbs said, "stay there and keep me informed."

One hour later Murray called to inform Hobbs that Davies had died.

At 9:00 am Hobbs had an incident room set up, and ten of his best officer's present and listening intently.

"At about 11:00 pm last night Chris Davies, an associate of Billy and Jack Maclaren, was shot three times in the face whilst sitting in a minicab, then the perpetrator, according to witnesses, made a reference to the Maclaren's before he drove off. Davies died a few hours later. Both Billy and Jack have since been seen surrounded by their heavies for protection, everything is pointing to the beginnings of a gang war. The only clue we have as to motive is that there is quite a large sum of money at stake."

"Anyone have any ideas?" Hobbs asked.

"I don't know if you heard guv, but the Crown got firebombed a couple of nights ago and whoever did it left a message on the wall stating that they wanted their money back," said one PC.

"OK, that's a start," Hobbs said. "You go down to the pub with Sgt. Murray and have a talk to the landlord to see if he can give us any clues," he said to the PC.

"The rest of you, I want you to talk to all of your informants and see if we can shed a bit more light on what's going on and report directly to me," Hobbs said.

The room emptied quickly, and Hobbs returned to his office with yet another cup of cold coffee.

Chapter 19

Billy was sitting at the table in his kitchen, surrounded by his best men.

"Someone will have to pay for this," he said, his eyes wild with anger. "Jack, have we got any news on this Razor bloke yet? I want him dead."

"He seems to be keeping a very low profile at the moment, but when he appears, we'll have him," Jack replied.

"OK," said Billy, "get some more people out there looking, he can't just vanish."

"What about this Bobby fella, why aren't we out looking for him?" asked one of the heavies.

"Because I want that bastard for myself," Billy replied. As he said this, his phone started to ring.

"Hello," he said sternly.

"Billy," the voice said. "So sorry to hear about your mate Chris," he continued in a very sarcastic tone.

"Who the fuck is that?" Billy demanded.

"It's me, Billy," he replied, "It's Bobby."

"You cunt. I swear I am going to fucking kill you."

"Yes Billy, you keep saying that, but you haven't got anywhere near me yet," said Bobby. "Now seeing as what happened to your mate Chris you must now be aware that you're out of your league son. So why don't you just fuck off and leave me and my brother alone."

"I will not rest until I have my money back and you two scumbags are fucking dead," Billy told him.

"Well, that's not very nice is it," Bobby said, laughing "I'll just have to have another of your friends killed in the hope that you see sense."

Bobby terminated the call and turned to Razor smiling.

"I think we've got him rattled."

Razor laughed and looked over at James, who was sitting very quietly.

"This is all getting a bit out hand now Bobby," he said to his big brother. "I wish I'd never found that fucking envelope."

"Yes, but you did James and I did warn you that things would get rough," Bobby told him.

"But I didn't really think people would get killed," James replied.

"For the amount of money, we're talking about I would think a few more bodies will turn up before it's finished," Bobby said nonchalantly.

"Anyway, as soon as all this is over me and Lisa are going abroad," James said, "I just need to get Lisa's passport from the house."

"OK, I'll get someone to go over there and pick it up, give me your keys," Bobby said.

"Can't I go as well?" asked James.

"I don't think that would be a good idea," said Razor "They may well be watching the place," he added.

"That's true, James, give the keys to Razor, and he'll find someone to go and collect anything you want," said Bobby.

Reluctantly James gave his keys to Razor.

Razor rose from his chair, "I need to go now," he said, "Got a few things to sort out, I'll bring Lisa's passport over tonight."

"OK, keep in touch," Bobby said.

Razor left the two brothers alone.

"I'm actually getting quite scared now," James said.

"I thought you would be," Bobby said. "You've got to stand up for the family James, you need to understand that the Bolton's used to be a big name in London. I've had to build up the family name after Dad ruined it."

"What do you mean?" asked James with a puzzled expression.

"James, you know very little about our dad, he was an arsehole who did nothing for the family," he said. "He was a drunk and a womanizer. All the respect and money the family had built up over years of planning and scheming was frittered away," he continued. "Dad became a laughingstock."

"Is that why you left?" James asked.

"Partly," Bobby replied, "I knew I had it in me to make it big and become very wealthy, but I couldn't do it around here because of Dad's reputation."

"But he was good to Mum," James said.

"Only after I had him threatened," Bobby replied.

James was finding this information hard to take in. He had always thought of his father as quite a decent bloke who did everything to try and look after his family, and now he was being told he was a failed villain and a drunk.

"But what about the money he left for Mum when he died?" asked James.

"Dad was skint when he died," Bobby said, "It was me who gave Mum the money, to this day she still thinks Dad had saved it up for her. But he didn't."

"I can't believe it," said James.

"Mum never needs to know any of this," Bobby said to his little brother.

"No, of course not," James replied.

***

Razor spent the morning sorting out bits of business. Collecting a few pounds here and there a quick meeting in a pub with a few of the lads to make sure Frank had been hidden away somewhere and had all he needed. With just about everything done, he was about to return over to North London when he remembered the passport.

"Oh shit!" he said out loud.

"What's the problem?" asked Danny. Danny was quite new to the firm but had shown himself to be a good man to have on your side. A willing soldier. He, like Bobby, was originally from South of the river but had crossed over due to some trouble he had found himself in.

"I was supposed to be getting someone to go over to collect Lisa's passport from the house," Razor replied. "We'll have to go back over there."

"Leave it out," Danny said, "I've got to meet my bird in forty minutes, we'll never make it there and back in time."

"Is it something important?" Razor asked him.

"Yes, it is, we've got the rehearsal for the wedding next week," he replied.

Razor let out a big sigh. "OK, then I'll drop you at a station and go over on my own," he said.

"But Bobby said you were not to be left alone," Danny reminded him.

"I'm a big boy Danny," he said. "I think I'll be OK."

Razor dropped Danny at the next train station they saw and continued back into South London.

As he drove towards James house, he tried to phone Bobby. After six rings, the phone went to voice mail. Having listened to the message Razor spoke into the phone, "Forgot to go over to James house, I'm on my own now can you try and send me over some back up just in case. Cheers mate."

Razor arrived outside the house, and all looked very quiet. He drove up and down the road looking for either someone who Bobby had sent or for some of Maclarens men plotted up waiting for James to reappear. There was no one. He tried to call Bobby and got the answerphone again. After taking one more look along the road, he decided to go in. He parked his vehicle and got out, as he entered the front garden, he had another look around him. Still, there was no one to be seen. He reached into his pocket and retrieved the key that James had given him, walked to the door and inserted it into the lock. He slowly pushed the door, and apart from a few days post, there was no resistance. Razor carried on inside and into the kitchen, he turned the light on, and as he did, he looked ahead of him towards the window. In the reflection of the window, he could see a figure behind him. He turned as quickly as he could, but he was too slow. The heavy end of a tyre lever caught him on the side of the head. He started to throw wild punches connecting with a couple but suddenly realised there wasn't just one attacker there was at least three. He felt another solid blow to his head, and as he went down, he could feel kicks coming in from all angles.

The next thing Razor knew was that he was seated upright and tied to a chair in the centre of the kitchen. He opened his eyes and looked around him there were two more people here now one of which was Pete Maclaren who they had kidnapped a few days earlier.

"This is him," Pete was saying, "This is the one they call Razor," A big man was staring at Razor.

"Are you sure this is him?" Jack asked his brother without taking his eyes from Razor.

"Definite," Pete answered.

"I thought you were supposed to be a bit tasty?" Jack said, laughing at Razor.

"You must be Jack?" Razor said sarcastically.

"That's right," Jack said, "I've been looking forward to this," he continued, "I am gonna kick your arse big time."

"OK, untie me and me, and you can go for it," Razor said.

Jack started to laugh, "Why would I want to do that?" he asked, delivering a huge right hook to the side of Razor's head. The chair rocked, but a determined Razor stayed upright. "I want a few answers from you before I finish you off, you cunt," Jack said, "Where's that little shit with all our money?" Razor just smiled as Jack threw another huge punch into the centre of his face. Razor felt his nose shatter as the punch landed but just sat there resolute till the end.

After twenty minutes of questioning, Jack was getting frustrated, he pulled a knife from his pocket, opened the blade and locked it.

"Couldn't do it with your fists then?" Razor mumbled through swollen and bleeding lips, "it's like being punched by a girl."

Jack completely lost it at this point and with his knife in hand, approached Razor and sliced the bottom half of his left ear clean off. Razor let out a huge scream, and his head dropped forward as blood started pulsing from the wound on the side of his head.

"This is your last chance, you cunt," Jack screamed, "where's our fucking money?"

"Go fuck yourself, Jack," Razor replied.

With that, Jack let out a huge roar and rushing forward he held Razor's head back and plunged the knife deep into Razor's left eye. He let out a gurgling scream, and his head fell further back as the knife was pushed in up to the hilt.

"Quick let's get the fuck out of here," one of Jack's guys called to him. Jack tried to retrieve the knife but couldn't free it from the bone and muscle it had immersed itself in.

They made a quick exit from the house, jumped into two waiting cars and sped off.

***

James and Bobby were at the hospital sitting with Terry when the nurse came in.

"I'm afraid you'll have to leave now, gentlemen," she told them. "Terry needs some rest."

Terry was coming on well, but the doctors were still concerned about a couple of the head blows he had received and were determined to keep him in for a while longer.

James and Bobby said their goodbye's and left the room.

"Fancy a pint?" Bobby asked James.

"Sounds good to me," he replied.

They left the hospital and got into James new car. As they did, Bobby remembered he had turned his phone off whilst in the hospital and turned it back on. An array of messages came flooding through making ringing and buzzing noises as they did. Bobby noticed a couple of missed calls from Razor and a new voice mail message. He scrolled through his contacts until he found Razor and pressed the call button, the phone rang and rang without being answered.

"That's strange," Bobby said, "I can't get hold of Razor." Bobby went into his voice mail, "You have one new message!" the voice told him. He pressed the button to retrieve the message, as he listened, James saw a look of panic appear on his face. He slammed the phone down and shouted at James "Your house now, let's go!"

As they were travelling Bobby made call after call, asking everyone if they had seen or heard from Razor, no one had. Everyone who he had spoken to were ordered to meet them at James house ASAP.

As they pulled into the street, all looked quiet. James noticed three men in a car, and as they slowly drove past, Bobby recognised them as his blokes. They parked up the car and walked towards the house. When they were in the front garden, Bobby instructed two of them to go down the side path to the rear of the house. As they arrived at the front door, they noticed it was slightly open.

"You wait here," Bobby instructed James as he beckoned the other man to enter the house with him.

Bobby entered the hallway and could see that the only light on was in the kitchen, he headed towards the door with a baseball bat in his hand. He pushed open the door and let out a scream of anger. Razor was sitting tied to a chair with blood still seeping from his ear, and the knife still protruding from his eye socket. He ran towards his best friend.

"Razor," he said, "Razor," he repeated. As he got closer Razor turned his head very slightly.

"It was Jack," he whispered to Bobby, "Kill that bastard for me."

"I will Razor," Bobby replied, "I promise you I will."

Razor's head dropped forward as he took his last breath and Bobby just stood in front of him staring at the bloody mess which was formerly his best friend.

"Let's get out," he ordered. As everyone left Bobby turned to take one final look at his mate. As he turned away out of the corner of his eye, he saw the passport on the kitchen side, and he picked it up and put it in his pocket.

They got back into the cars and were gone. As they drove Bobby's phone rang once again, he answered it.

"Your turn to lose your best mate now, Bobby," Billy's voice said, "Not nice is it?"

"You fucking wanker Maclaren," Bobby said, "you tell your brother from me that he will never be safe anywhere he goes, and I don't care how far this goes you will never see that money you cunt!" The call was ended abruptly.

Chapter 20

DI Hobbs arrived at the crime scene as they were removing Razor from the chair.

Here we go, thought Hobbs it's all starting to kick off now. "Do we know who he is yet?" Hobbs asked one of the uniformed officers.

"His name is Ian Richards," he told the DI.

"OK, get him to the lab and ask them to fingerprint him first and see if we can find anything else out about him, the name means nothing to me."

"No, nor me," the PC replied.

Hobbs took his phone out and dialled a number.

"Hello Murray, we've got another one," he said, "tied to a chair with a knife in his eye."

"Nice," said Murray.

"See if you can find out where the Maclarens have been all night," Hobbs instructed him.

"OK, guv, I'll see you back at the station," he replied.

Just over an hour later, Hobbs was sitting at his desk with yet another cup of lukewarm coffee when he heard a knock at the door.

"Come in!"

Sgt. Murray entered the room with one of the young DC's, and they both took a seat.

"What have you got for me?" Hobbs asked.

"Billy has an alibi he was in a restaurant all evening with his wife," he said, "our boys were sitting outside and followed him home, and he's still there now."

"OK, what about Jack?" Hobbs asked.

"The boys followed him to a pub, and they sat outside all evening," Murray said, "after you called me one of our guys went inside just to make sure, and Jack and a couple of his blokes were nowhere to be seen."

"What?" shouted Hobbs, "You lost him in a fucking pub, why didn't we have someone stationed at the back entrance?"

"In fairness to the lads, there is no back entrance for the general public," he informed his DI, "the landlord must have let him out through the private accommodation."

"OK, someone get down there and talk to the landlord and find out what time he left," said Hobbs, "By the way what happened at the other pub with the graffiti?" he asked.

"The landlord there wasn't very forthcoming, but a snout of mine reckons whoever owes the Maclarens money drinks in that boozer," Murray told him.

"That's strange," said Hobbs, "I didn't have that pub associated with anyone big time."

"No, neither did I," agreed Murray.

"Hey what about that Terry Alleyne?" said Hobbs, "I know he's only small-time, but he does have dealings with the Maclarens, and he drinks in the Crown," he added.

"Good point," Murray agreed, "We'll pull him in for a chat." There was another knock on the door.

"Come in," called Hobbs. A uniformed officer entered the room carrying a file of papers.

"Been asked to bring this up from the lab," he said.

"Thanks," said Murray taking the file as the PC left the room. Murray passed the file to Hobbs who opened it up and started reading it.

"We've got a match for our man," he told them, "Ian Richards."

"Well we knew that," said Murray.

"Wait a minute," said Hobbs, "He's also known as Razor and has a record as long as your arm."

"Razor Richards," said the DC, "I nicked him once over in Holloway when I was stationed over that way."

"Well, who is he?" asked Hobbs.

"He was the right-hand man to Bobby Bolton," he said. "Oh, fuck me," said Hobbs, "Bobby fucking Bolton. Now we're getting into the heavy stuff."

"Bobby, who?" asked Murray.

"He's one hard bastard," Hobbs told him, "the Maclarens may have opened a can of worms here."

"What's he doing on this side of the water?" asked Murray. "That's the big question," replied Hobbs, "we need to find a connection between Bolton, the Maclarens and the Crown pub."

"OK, first thing in the morning I need someone to go and lean on both of those pub landlords and Murray, you can pick up Terry Alleyne and bring him in for a friendly chat," said Hobbs.

At 9:00 am the following morning, Murray was on the phone trying to track down Terry. He got the same answer from everybody. "Not seen him in about a week." *Very strange*, he thought.

In an attempt to kill two birds with one stone, he decided to go to the Crown and have a word with the landlord. When he arrived at the pub, Geoff was standing outside with two men wearing suits and carrying briefcases.

"Morning, Geoff," he said, "can we have a little chat?"

"Hi Colin, I'm just talking to the guys from the insurance company," he said, "I'll be with you in five minutes."

DS Murray lit a cigarette as he waited. He looked around the outside of the building and saw the graffiti on the wall. He tried to see through the window, but all he could make out was darkness, he pushed open the door and looked inside. Everything was ruined, what wasn't burnt was soaked and totally unusable. From the carpets to the light fittings, everything would have to go.

"All right, Colin," said Geoff, "what can I do for you?"

"I'm a bit confused, Geoff, who of your regular customers would be stupid enough to owe money to the Maclaren's?" he asked.

"I honestly don't know," Geoff replied.

"Well they've left a message on the wall of your pub, and I'm guessing it's not you who owes them money," Murray said, "so my guess is that they think you know who does."

Geoff was starting to look very uncomfortable. He looked around at the people wandering in and out of the station and with a nervous look on his face he whispered to DS Murray. "Let's go upstairs, I don't really want to be seen with you out here."

"Fair enough," Murray said.

They entered the pub, and the stench of burning and damp hung in the air. They passed through the hatch in the bar and up the stairs to the private accommodation.

"Coffee?" Geoff asked.

"Sounds good," said Murray, "Milk and two sugars, please." While Geoff was in the kitchen, Murray looked around the small but very tidy living room.

There was a large bookcase spilling over with all kinds of books from horror to romance. The only thing that was missing was a woman's touch.

Geoff came back with the coffee.

"Please take a seat," he said to DS Murray.

Murray sat down and placed his coffee on a small table in front of him and sat back.

"So, what can you tell me, Geoff?" he asked.

"This is totally off the record, OK?" Geoff said.

"We'll have to see what you've got first," Murray said. "The Maclaren' have been coming in lately, asking if anyone had been flashing a lot of money around," he told him.

"And had anyone?" Murray asked.

"Not huge amounts," Geoff answered.

"But some, yes."

"Well, there is one guy," said Geoff, "He's not spent fortunes, but it certainly seemed like his luck had changed."

"And who is this?" Murray enquired.

"His name is James," Geoff told him, "He usually comes in, and although he drinks with mates, he usually buys just his own drinks and doesn't get involved in big rounds."

"But that's changed, has it?" asked Murray.

"As I said, he's not spent a fortune, but he's certainly been a bit more generous than usual," he said, "and he appears not to have been going to work either."

"How do you know that?" Murray ventured.

"His mate who he works with came in looking for him," Geoff said, "in fact quite a few people have been in here lately, looking for him."

"Really, like who?"

"Well, Terry was looking for him," he said.

"Terry Alleyne?" Murray asked.

"Yes, and look what happened to him," Geoff said.

"What happened to Terry?"

"I thought you would have heard," he said, "he got badly beaten up just around the corner."

"By who?" asked Murray.

"I saw nothing," Geoff said.

"Was it the Maclarens Geoff?" Murray asked.

Geoff just turned his head and stared towards the window. "I'll take that as a yes then," Murray said, "what did he do to deserve it?"

"I don't know, but I think it's connected to this money," Geoff told him.

"Do you know where he is now?" Murray asked.

"Hospital apparently," Geoff answered.

"So, if I'm getting this right some bloke called James, appears to have come into some money that the Maclarens think is theirs," said Murray, "and Terry had a hiding for it."

"That's about right," said Geoff.

"You said other people came looking for this James guy, who was that?" Murray asked.

"He was a great big bloke," Geoff said, "he claimed to be James brother."

"What was his name?" asked Murray.

"I can't remember," said Geoff, "I wrote it down somewhere with his phone number."

"Have you still got it by any chance?" Murray asked.

"No, I gave it to Lisa," he said.

"Who's Lisa?"

"Lisa is sort of James girlfriend," he told him, "they share a house just around the corner, but recently it seems like they're getting a bit closer," he continued, "actually I haven't seen her around lately either, come to think of it."

"So, James, Lisa and Terry have all gone missing after the Maclarens started asking questions about them?" Murray said.

"Yes," replied Geoff.

"Seems a little suspicious, don't you think?" Murray asked.

"Bobby," said Geoff.

"What?" Murray asked, looking puzzled.

"Bobby was the name of the bloke who said he was James brother," Geoff said.

"What is James surname," Murray asked.

"I'm not sure, but I have it somewhere," Geoff said, "he registered for the darts team last year his name will be on the registration form."

"That's great," Murray replied, "where is it?"

"I don't know I'll have to search around for it," he said, "Can I call you when I find it?" he asked.

"OK," said Murray handing Geoff one of his business cards, "I need it as soon as possible Geoff."

"I'll let you know today," he assured him.

Murray drained his cup and stood up. The two men shook hands, and DS Murray left.

When he got to his car, he called Hobbs.

"Hello Guv," he said, "there are certainly a few strange things going on down at The Crown."

"Really," Hobbs answered, "like what?"

"Billy Maclaren has been asking questions, a couple of people seem to have disappeared, and Terry Alleyne got bloody good hiding," he told him.

"OK Colin," said Hobbs, "you keep digging and let me know what you find later, I've got a couple of people to talk to, I'll be in the office about three o'clock."

"I'll see you there," Murray replied.

Chapter 21

Billy Maclaren was holding court in the Kings Head pub. He had two men situated in cars outside each entrance and plenty of support inside the pub if required.

"Things are going to get even worse now," he informed his assorted troops. "We got them back for Chris' death last night, and they are likely to come at us with everything now," he continued, "don't any of you go anywhere on your own and make sure somebody on the firm knows where you are at all times. This is going to be very nasty, but I can assure you all that the rewards will be worth it."

"What is the plan now, Billy?" one of them asked.

"I don't think we should wait for them to strike back," Billy said, "I think we should get on and finish this quickly, we need to find the younger brother first, he's the one who has the money, once we've got him Bobby will have to give up. We need to be on the front foot."

The door of the pub opened, and every head turned, as the man walked towards the crowd. Billy rose from his chair and walked towards him.

"Detective Inspector Hobbs," Billy exclaimed, "to what do we owe this unexpected pleasure?"

"Hello Billy," Hobbs said, "I think you know why I'm here; we need to talk."

Billy walked towards a small table in the corner of the bar.

"A large Jack Daniels for my friend, please," Billy called to the barman as they sat at the table. The drink appeared at the table in seconds.

"So, Billy you've gone after the big fish this time," Hobbs said.

"They called it on," said Billy, "They stole my money."

"Is this money really worth the two lives that have already been lost? How much is it?" he asked.

"Oh, only the small matter of seventy-two million quid," Billy told him and started to laugh as he saw the look on Hobbs' face.

"Shit," was all that Hobbs could think to say. "How the fuck could they take that sort of money off you?" he asked.

"I don't want to go into that," Billy said, "What I would like to explain to you is that in the past we have worked well together you and I and I've always looked after you. Help me sort this one out, and you will be able to retire early."

"I don't know what I can do," replied Hobbs.

"Just point me in the right direction, and I'll do the rest," Billy said.

"Leave it to me," Hobbs replied.

Hobbs necked his JD, and as he walked out of the pub, he stopped and turned towards Billy, "I hope whoever did your dirty work last night was wearing gloves because they left the knife in his eye." Billy's eyes shot towards Jack, who was looking down at the floor.

"The knife will be in the lab for analysis today," he said as he left the pub.

Hobbs was laughing to himself as he started the engine and pulled away. He knew there was no chance of getting any prints off the knife because the handle was too soaked in blood, but from the way, Billy reacted he now almost certainly knew that it was Jack who had done it.

Hobbs arrived at the station at twelve minutes past three, and all his team were in the incident room waiting. "OK, ladies and gentlemen, what have we got?"

DS Murray stood up and gave Hobbs all the details of his chat with Geoff at the Crown. This was followed by an account from a rather embarrassed DC as to how they had managed to lose Jack Maclaren the night before and the fact that the landlord of the pub denied having let him out of the back entrance. Murray's phone rang and Hobbs glared at him. He looked at the screen on his phone.

"Sorry, Guv," he said, "I've got to take this, it could be relevant," Murray answered his phone and after a couple of OKs and a thank you, he hung up.

"The plot thickens," said Murray. "That was Geoff from the Crown, our person of interest, James, has the surname Bolton," he informed them.

"Bobby's brother," said Hobbs.

"Exactly," Murray replied.

"Do we have any idea where James is?" asked Hobbs. "None at all," Murray answered. "We can get a check put on his bank account and credit cards now though, if he uses them anywhere, we will know."

"Someone get on that straightaway," Hobbs said.

"What about Terry Alleyne?" Hobbs asked.

A young female DC stood up.

"I've checked all the hospitals and discovered he was taken to St. George's."

"Great, someone get down there and speak to him," said Hobbs.

"Sir," the young DC interrupted him, "He's no longer there, he was released into the care of a solicitor and sent to a private hospital," she told him, "I have been on the phone to all the private hospitals locally, and they either don't have him there, or they won't tell us."

"Who was the solicitor?" Hobbs asked.

"Again, they won't say," she replied.

"OK, I want 24-hour surveillance on the Maclarens, and we need to find Bobby Bolton so we can keep an eye on him. Murray, you sort out who's doing what and then come and see me in my office," Hobbs left the incident room and went to the canteen.

He got himself a coffee and returned to his office. On the way, he heard someone call his name.

"John, John!"

Hobbs turned around to see the Detective Chief Inspector coming down the corridor towards him.

"Hello, sir," Hobbs said.

"I hear you've got a big case started up," he said.

"Yes," replied Hobbs, "looks like a gang war."

"So I hear," the DCI replied, "any resources you need just let me know," he said, "I don't want these scumbags running around my manor killing each other."

"I'll let you know if I need anything, sir," Hobbs replied.

"Come to my office at eleven o'clock tomorrow morning for a full briefing," he ordered.

"Will do, sir."

Hobbs continued down the corridor, entered his office and sat at his desk. He took his phone from his pocket and dialled a number.

"Hello mate," Hobbs said, "It's been a long time."

DS Murray was busy allocating people to different jobs and making sure every base was covered. As he looked up at the board in the incident room, the two glaring omissions were the photographs of the Bolton brothers. All the other major players were there. There was however still no clue as to why a small-time no one like James Bolton was in debt to the Maclarens.

Fifteen minutes later Murray went to Hobbs' office and knocked lightly on the door.

"Come in!" called Hobbs.

Hobbs and Murray spent an hour discussing what they did and didn't know about the case, and it appeared they still knew very little.

It was just after five when Murray left to go and check on the surveillance teams watching the Maclarens and Hobbs was again left alone in his office.

Hobbs dialled a number on his phone, and after three rings, it was answered.

"Hello Billy," Hobbs said, "you already owe me one."

"For what?" asked Billy.

"That stupid shit of a brother of yours left his prints all over the knife," Hobbs said.

"You're kidding me," Billy replied.

"How else would I know it was him?" Hobbs asked.

"That's true," said Billy, "so what's happening now?" he asked.

"Well, I'll have to make it disappear, won't I," Hobbs told him.

"I'll look after you for this," Billy promised.

"Make sure you do," said Hobbs as he disconnected the call.

***

Hobbs left the office at six-thirty and drove through the busy rush hour streets of South London crossing the Thames via Tower Bridge.

He continued along Commercial Street and on towards Shoreditch. The streets on the north side of the river seemed darker and colder, and the buildings looked aged and weary. He parked his car in a small side street, and after feeding the parking meter, he walked around the corner and headed towards the Royal Oak pub which stood at the end of the road. As he got closer, he noticed a couple of heavy-looking men standing on the corner. He passed by them and entered the pub. There were only about ten people in the pub, all of them male, and all looked like they had done their fair share of prison time. Hobbs walked to the bar.

"Jack Daniels, please," he said to the barman.

"I'll get that," a voice from the other end of the bar called.

Hobbs turned to see the smiling face of Bobby Bolton "How are you doing, John?" he asked as he walked down the bar to join the Detective Inspector.

"I'm OK," Hobbs answered, "And you?" he inquired.

"I'm good," Bobby told him.

DI Hobbs and Bobby Bolton had known each other for many years. Hobbs had been a friend of Teddy Bayliss, Bobby's mentor, and they had first met when Bobby was about seventeen. Hobbs and Teddy did favours for each other, and although Bobby had never asked, he liked to think that he could call on Hobbs if he needed too. Bobby, however, never forgot the lesson he learned from Teddy that 'a bent copper was only on your side until a better deal came along'.

"What I would really like to know is how your brother is doing," Hobbs said.

Bobby started laughing. "When you called I kind of guessed this wasn't just going to be a drink for old time's sake," he said, "let's go and find a table."

They walked to the nearest table and sat down.

"What the fuck is going on, Bobby?" Hobbs asked.

"I'm not sure what you mean," Bobby replied.

"As you are no doubt aware, I'm posted in South London these days, and I have a problem with wannabe gangster's going around killing each other," Hobbs said, "and I'm getting proper pissed off with it Bobby."

"What does this have to do with me?" Bobby asked.

"Don't fuck with me, Bobby," he said, "if you don't know what I'm talking about, let me ask your mate Razor, is he here?"

"No," replied Bobby staring at the floor of the pub.

"Exactly," Hobbs said, "because he's in the mortuary with a fucking knife in his eye."

The rest of the pub had now gone very quiet.

"Now get your fucking act in gear Bobby and give them their money back or you'll have me and the Maclarens to worry about," Hobbs said in a raised voice. With that, he finished his drink and left the pub.

One hour later, whilst watching TV at home, Billy's phone rang. "Hello," he said.

"Hi Billy," a voice the other end said, "I have it from a very good source that Hobbs went to see Bobby Bolton tonight and warned him against carrying this thing on," he said, "he actually made it sound like he was on your side."

"Thanks, mate, that's good to know," Billy replied as he hung up the phone.

Chapter 22

It was Saturday morning, and Jack woke early. He looked alongside him to see a young blonde woman who didn't look quite as young and pretty as she had the night before. He raised the duvet and slapped her hard on the backside, and she woke with a jump.

"Jack, you bastard," she said, "why must you do that?" she asked. Jack just laughed.

"Look what I've got for you," he said, pulling the duvet back to reveal his erect manhood.

"You can fuck right off," she said. She climbed off the bed and pulled one of Jack's sweatshirts on to cover her nudity.

"Do you want a cup of tea?" she asked him.

"Yes, two sugars please," he replied as he also climbed from the bed and headed for the en-suite bathroom.

Marie had been in an on and off relationship with Jack since she was sixteen and she was now 28. She had a lot of feelings for him but would never commit because of his hell-raising ways and his terrible temper. She was also aware that he wasn't in any way faithful to her. He spoilt her with presents and paid the rent on her one-bedroom flat, but in all the years they had been seeing each other he had never told her he loved her, and she had never been allowed to meet his mother. Despite all this and totally unbeknown to her, he was actually very much in love with her. Still, he could never show it as he considered it a sign of weakness.

When he finished showering, he put on his bathroom robe and went and joined Marie in the kitchen.

"Where's my tea?" he asked as he sat at the kitchen table. "Jack, there's no bloody milk'," she said, "go and get some," she told him.

"I've got no time," he told her, "I'm meeting Billy, you go and get it while I get dressed, and I'll just about have time for a cuppa before I go," he said.

144

"You are one lazy bastard," she told him.

Jack gave her a big cheesy smile and put his arms around her. "I'll make you a bacon sandwich while you're getting the milk," he said.

"OK, but you'll have to move your car first, or I won't be able to get out," she said.

Picking his car keys up from the kitchen side, he threw them to her.

"Take mine," he said. As Marie ran upstairs to find some clothes Jack opened the fridge and reached inside for the bacon, he put the frying pan on the hob and after putting some cooking oil into the pan turned on the gas. Marie reappeared in the kitchen. She was dressed and had pushed her hair up on top of her head.

"I hope no one sees me looking like this," she said.

"You look gorgeous," Jack said. Marie just looked at him.

"Was that a compliment," she said, laughing.

"Piss off," replied Jack.

Marie opened the front door and walked along the gravel pathway, which led to the drive she pressed the button on the key fob, and the lights flashed on Jack's Jaguar. She opened the door, sat in the car and put the key in the ignition and turned it.

Jack heard the explosion and felt the entire house shake. He rushed out to the front door, which had been blown off its hinges by the blast, and out towards the burning wreck that was once his car. He tried to get closer to the car, screaming out Marie's name but all in vain. He could faintly hear sirens in the distance, but they would never arrive in time to save her, he knew that.

He looked to the sky and screamed, for the first time in his life, he actually felt true pain, and he could feel tears welling up in his eyes. He collapsed to the floor and just lay there.

The fire engine pulled up six minutes later, and the fire was extinguished within a couple of minutes. The paramedics stood around knowing their presence there wasn't actually needed as this was a case for the coroner's undertakers. Jack retrieved his phone from the kitchen and called Billy. He explained to Billy what had happened.

Billy had never heard his brother cry before and was in his car and on his way over to him as they were still talking. He arrived ten minutes later, the sight of the burnt-out Jaguar and the smell of fuel and death in the air turned his stomach. He went into the house and found Jack sitting on the sofa with a large scotch in his hand and staring at a cartoon on the TV. He turned the volume down and sat next to his brother. They sat in silence for some minutes until they heard a voice coming from the front door.

"Hello, is it ok to come in?" called DI Hobbs.

Billy went to the door and brought Hobbs through to the living room where Jack sat, still in his bathrobe.

"I'm very sorry for your loss Jack," Hobbs said.

"Billy, get him out of here," Jack replied in a whisper.

Billy took Hobbs into the kitchen and explained exactly what had occurred there that morning. He also told Hobbs that Bobby Bolton was as good as dead.

"Let's get your money back then we can throw him to the wolves," Hobbs said.

***

Bobby was eating his breakfast when there was a knock at his door. He stood and crossed the kitchen and through the hallway to the front door. He opened the door and saw Frank standing there, looking grim.

"Hi Frank," he said, "what's up?" he asked, noticing that Frank was not acting his normal self.

"We hit Jack's car this morning," Frank said.

"Is he dead?" smiled Bobby.

"Sadly, no, he isn't."

"Who fucked up then?" he asked, "that bomb should have killed anyone in the car."

"Yes, it did," Frank replied, "only it wasn't Jack."

"Shit, who was it then?" asked Bobby.

"It was his girlfriend," he was informed.

"Oh fuck," he said, "I take it she's dead?" Bobby inquired.

"Of course, she's fucking dead, the fucking car blew up as she started it," Frank said getting very pissed of now. "This is getting out of hand, Bobby."

"Yes Frank, this wasn't meant to happen," he told him "get some more people guarding Lisa just in case."

"Will do," said Frank as he turned to leave.

Bobby walked back into his kitchen and picked up the phone that he used to contact Billy. He looked at the phone for a few minutes then started typing.

The phone vibrated in Billy's pocket. He looked to see there was a text message. He opened it.

THAT WASN'T MEANT TO HAPPEN
IT SHOULD HAVE BEEN JACK
IT CHANGES NOTHING BETWEEN US
BUT PLEASE PASS MY CONDOLENCES TO
THE GIRL'S FAMILY.
BOBBY

Bobby couldn't finish his breakfast.

He phoned James and told him the news.

"This has got to stop," James told him. "I'm not sure it's worth the money," he said.

"Unfortunately, James, this isn't just about the money anymore," Bobby said, "It's gone too far to walk away now."

"Do you think Jack will go after Lisa again?" James asked.

"I have no doubt that he will," Bobby told him, "So we may have to keep moving her."

"She won't like that," James replied.

"If she wants to stay alive, she'll just have to put up with it," said Bobby. "Give her a call and see if there's anywhere else, she can go."

"OK," said James.

James came off the phone and sat quietly in reflection of what Bobby had just told him. After a few seconds, he could feel tears welling up in his eyes. It had seemed such a good result for him when he found the envelope, he had a few extra quid in his pocket and had enjoyed being able to throw it about a bit. Then they found the lottery ticket. He wished now he had just thrown it away instead of letting Lisa check it. The whole thing had caused nothing but trouble. Three people had died, and he and Lisa were miles apart, and he was scared for both of their lives. He realised that, although it was great to have him back in his life, he was nothing like his brother. He could remember he and Robert (as he was known then) playing together as kids and although he was never nasty, Robert always had to win. It seemed to James that they were now playing another game that Robert was determined not to lose. Unfortunately, the stakes were a lot higher in this game.

Bobby and James met as arranged at a restaurant in St. Katherine's Dock for lunch. Bobby had a couple of his boys posted outside to keep an eye on things, and as much as James liked Frank, he was getting fed up not being able to go anywhere without him like his shadow.

They sat at their table and ordered from the menu.

"Not hungry bruv?" Bobby asked, noticing James had only ordered a side salad.

"No, I seem to have lost my appetite," he answered. As James was about to tell Bobby of his worries and fears about the whole situation, Bobby's phone rang.

"Hello," Bobby said.

"You fucking scum!" screamed Billy. "You kill my brother's girl and then send me a fucking text message."

"I meant what I said in the message," Bobby told him. "I'm very sorry the girl died she wasn't the target."

"Yeah, well, you will be very sorry now because my next target is your mother," Billy told him.

"Don't even go there, Billy," Bobby shouted, "I thought it was me and my brother you wanted dead."

"I'm leaving you two until last so you can suffer like Jack is doing now," he hung up.

The restaurant had gone very quiet after Bobby's rant down the phone, and as he looked around at the other diners, they all turned away.

"James, I know you're feeling bad about what has happened, but that scum is now threatening Mum," he said.

"Does he know where she is?" James asked.

"I fucking hope not," Bobby replied. "I'll get her moved straight away."

It was very cold on the front at Brighton. Only a few pensioners wandering along taking in the bracing chilly wind as they went. The two men sat in the car with the heating at full blast trying to keep warm. A phone rang.

One of the men looked at the screen.

"It's Billy," he said to the man in the passenger seat.

"Hello," he said.

"Is everything sorted?" Billy asked.

"Yes, I spoke to one of the girls who work in the boarding house," he replied, "She's got a ground floor room at the front of the house, I saw the old girl go out this morning, and I'm just waiting for her to get back."

"OK," said Billy. "As soon as she's back, just do it."

"Will do."

The two men sat waiting patiently one playing solitaire on his phone the other watching in all directions. Another half an hour passed.

"Do you fancy a coffee?" one of the men asked.

"Billy said we must not leave here," he told him "Neither of us, I don't want to have to tell Billy we missed her, do you?"

"Well, where the fuck is she?" the other man said, turning off his game on the phone and sounding very bored.

"Wait!" said a very excited voice. "Here she comes."

An elderly woman was walking along the pavement towards the seafront boarding house carrying some shopping. She came to the stairs at the front of the house and after removing her gloves, fumbled through her pockets for the key. She pushed the key into the lock, opened the door and went in. "Right we've just got to give her time to get into her room," the man watching said.

They sat watching intently, waiting for a sign that she had entered the room. Suddenly they saw the net curtain move and a silhouetted figure moving around.

"Let's go," the man in the passenger seat shouted.

The driver slammed the car into gear and screeched across the road and stopped directly outside the house. They both jumped out of the car one carrying a short automatic assault rifle which burst into life, shattering the windows as it fired. The other man lit a rag which was pushed into a bottle of petrol and hurled it through the window. They ran back to the car and sped away.

The man in the passenger seat dialled a number on his phone.

"All done Billy," he said.

"Well done," Billy answered. "Now get rid of the car and disappear." He hung up.

Bobby and James had just finished lunch and were leaving the restaurant when Bobby received a text message.

THAT *WAS* MEANT TO HAPPEN.
FUCK YOU.

The colour drained from his face as he read the message.

"What the fuck is going on?" James asked.

Bobby was already dialling the number of the boarding house. It kept ringing. Eventually, an answerphone cut in and Bobby hung up.

"I think they've got to Mum," he said to James.

James just stared in disbelief at his elder brother.

"What the fuck have I done?" James said, "Take the fucking money and go," he said to Bobby. "I want nothing more to do with any of this."

Bobby's phone started to ring, and without looking at the screen, he answered it.

"Bloody good job you did of protecting me," the voice said. He had never in his life been so pleased to be told off by his mum. "Thank God," he said, "are you OK?" he asked.

"I am," she answered, "but the poor girl who was cleaning my room is in a bad way," she told him, "She got shot, but they managed to get her out before the fire took hold."

"The fire," exclaimed Bobby, "What exactly happened?" he asked.

Eileen explained in detail what had happened and that as she came in the nice girl who cleaned was just about to start in her room, so she decided to have a cup of tea in the lounge.

After she had given him all the details, he passed the phone to James. Whilst James and his mum spoke, Bobby took Frank's phone and made a call.

"Pick my mum up and start driving towards the West Country. I will phone you later," he hung up.

"How the fuck did they know where she was?" James asked his brother.

"I've no idea," Bobby answered, "but we need to find out!" James phone vibrated in his pocket.

"Hello."

"James its Gary your house is on fire," he told him. "Oh shit," he replied. "I'll be round soon," James came off the phone.

"We need to go," he told Bobby.

"Where?" he asked.

"My place, it's on fucking fire!" James told him.

"Don't go there," Bobby said, "I guarantee you the Maclarens have done this, and they'll be waiting there for us to show our faces."

"Fucking bastards," James said.

"Do you still want to give them the money back?" Bobby asked, "Fuck them," James replied.

***

"Hi Bobby," Kenny's voice filled the car via the hands-free system, "Can you talk at the moment?" he inquired. "Yes, mate," he replied, "there's only me and James here, what's up?"

"Have you got a young guy called Danny working for you?" he enquired.

"Yes," said Bobby, "Good lad originally from your side of the river?"

"That's him," Kenny said, "but I'm not so sure about the good lad."

"Why do you say that?" asked Bobby.

"Was he there when Hobbs came to see you?" he asked.

"Yes."

"Well, that conversation got back to Billy," Kenny told him.

"Doesn't necessarily mean it's him though," replied Bobby.

"OK, did Danny leave Razor to go to James house on his own?" asked Kenny.

"Yes."

"And did Danny take your mum down to Brighton?"

"Fuck it yes he did," Bobby said.

"Think about it mate, you've got a grass in your team," Kenny said.

"That little shit!" Bobby shouted.

After thanking Kenny for the information, he hung up.

"I can't believe that little shit is stitching us up," James said.

"Yeah, it's not good," Bobby replied, "but meanwhile we can just feed him some shit and let him pass it on to Billy."

"This could work to our advantage," James said, smiling. "It will do for now, and when this is all over, we can send young Danny a little calling card," he laughed.

Billy was sitting in the King's Head with some of his boy's still smarting over what had happened to Jack's girl but feeling very smug about his retaliation when the door opened, and DI Hobbs walked in. He made his way to the table where Billy was sitting and pulled up a chair.

"This is getting out of hand," he told Billy.

"Fuck them," he replied, "They killed my brother's girl, so we went after his mum, I told you at the start they called it on," Billy said, "I bet they wished they hadn't fucking messed with me now."

"I think you should know Billy that all you managed to do in Brighton was set light to a boarding house, frighten a few old ladies and shoot the chambermaid. Bobby's mum was sitting at the back of the house having a cup of tea," he told Billy. "They've moved her now and I doubt you'll ever find out where she is."

"For fuck's sake," said Billy looking upwards as if to heaven "Can I not trust anyone to do anything right?" he slammed his fist onto the table.

"Right Billy leave this to me for now," Hobbs said, "I'm going to talk to Bobby and see if we can find some way to sort this out," he told him "In the meantime, I'll try and find out where they've put mum and the girlfriend just in case you need to know."

"Good man," Billy replied, "you will be well rewarded," he told him.

Chapter 23

A few hours later, after making sure it was all clear, James and Frank went around to what was left of what James used to call home. The entire place was wrecked. According to reports, the place went up in flames in no time at all. Gary had heard the firefighters talking, and they seemed to think that the fire had started at the front and back of the house at the same time, meaning that two petrol bombs were most likely used simultaneously.

James thought, *he had better phone Lisa and let her know the bad news.*

"Hi honey," James said as Lisa answered the phone. "James, what's happening?" she answered, "It seems like ages since we spoke."

"I'm sorry," he replied, "It's been a bit busy down here," he continued.

"Are you ok?" she asked.

"I'm fine," he assured her, "However, there is one thing I need to tell you."

"What, what's happened?" she asked.

"I'm afraid someone has set light to our house."

"Oh my God," she said, "Is it bad?"

"I'm afraid the whole place has been destroyed," he informed her, "It was the Maclarens."

"This is getting totally out of hand now," she said, "you have to put a stop to this somehow," she told him.

"Bobby says it's too late now," James told her. "Just a few more days, and hopefully we can be away forever," he said trying to reassure her. "Oh, and by the way, I am going to send you a new phone number, keep it safe and if you see anything strange or unusual, call it straight away."

"Whose number is it?" she asked.

"It's some friends of Bobby's they are parked up near to where you are and can be there in seconds if needed," he told her.

"Why would anyone know that I'm here?" she asked.

"They probably don't, but just in case, there is someone nearby," he told her.

"I really don't like this," she said.

"You'll be fine," James said. "Honestly," he added.

James finished the call and continued driving towards Tower Bridge the traffic was very busy for Saturday lunchtime and getting through the Elephant & Castle took about twenty minutes. As he drove, he was listening to one of the London talk radio shows. They had just finished an hour on homelessness in the capital, and the news followed. During the news, they reported on a house fire that had been raging earlier in South London and the fact that the police thought that it may be a further retaliation attack that was making up a part of a gang war that appeared to be going on throughout the streets of the capital. James felt quite excited in a strange sort of way to know that they were talking about him and his brother but still very frightened. As he finally crossed Tower Bridge, he listened intently as an ex-copper was telling the radio show host how these things never end well. "Some of these feuds go on for years," he was saying, "and the only way of finishing it is for the top men to die." That thought shook James. To hear someone talking so matter of fact on a radio show about what was likely to happen to him was very disturbing.

About five minutes later, James pulled up outside the Royal Oak and parked. He entered the pub and made his way to the bar. Having ordered himself a pint, he went and joined his brother and some others at a table. He noticed that amongst their crowd was Danny, no doubt waiting for some snippet of information he could take back to the Maclarens.

As James sat down the door opened, and DI Hobbs entered the bar. He sauntered over to the table where they sat, and one of the boys gave up his chair for him.

"Evening Bobby."

"Good evening Detective Inspector," he replied, "and what can we do for you this evening?" Bobby asked.

"You need to sort this whole mess out with the Maclarens," he told him.

"That cunt tried to kill my mum today," Bobby said, "and you want me to forget it." He started to laugh.

"Bobby, this is getting way too heavy. If it carries on like this, I won't be able to turn the other eye any longer," he told him. "I really don't give a fuck," Bobby replied, "now if you can't help me then piss off."

DI Hobbs sat very quietly and shook his head, "You're a fool, Bobby, you will never win this fight."

Bobby flew out of his seat, and before Hobbs could move, he had hold of him by his throat.

"I can win any fight I choose," Bobby said his face just inches from Hobbs. "Now fuck off and tell your mate Billy to watch his fucking back cause I'm coming for him."

James sat rigid in his seat. He looked around the table as his brother released his grip on the detective and could see Danny staring at Hobbs.

"Danny," said Bobby. "See DI Hobbs off the premises and make sure he doesn't return."

The young lad looked very nervous as he tried to usher Hobbs out of the pub. He followed him out of the door, and when they were out of sight, Hobbs turned to Danny, "just find out anything you can," he whispered.

Danny nodded and watched as Hobbs disappeared around the corner.

"He's gone," he said as he returned into the pub.

"Well done, Danny," Bobby said, smiling at the youngster.

"Now fellas, on another point we have a job to do on Monday night," Bobby announced, "Me and Razor were planning this for about two months, and I think in his memory we should go ahead with it, there will be a nice few grand in it for each of you," which was met with smiles. "Now we need to meet at about seven on the third floor of the building on Mears Street, make sure you're tooled up," he said, "it'll be nice to take our minds of the Maclarens for a while."

As they all finished their drinks and started to disperse, Bobby was keeping a special eye on Danny.

Chapter 24

It was Monday afternoon, and Billy was in the King's Head with Jack and his most loyal soldiers.

"Tonight, is the night," he said, "I've had a tip-off that they are planning a job and will be at a building on Mears Street from about seven o'clock. We will be waiting for them."

"How are we getting in?" Jack asked.

"I've sweetened the security guard," he told him, "we must be there for six-thirty, so we're ahead of them."

"We will be leaving here at ten past six," he said, "if any of you haven't got the balls for it, don't bother turning up."

They all reassembled and left at precisely ten past six, not one of the gang failed to show. They travelled in three Transit vans. Twenty of them in all, every one of them properly tooled up. When they arrived at the building, they drove straight to the security gate, and the guard let them in. They parked the vans in a secluded area at the back of the site and made their way into the building.

"I was told they will be meeting on the third floor," Billy whispered as they climbed the stairs in silence. They came to the top of a flight of stairs with a large board displaying the number three.

"In we go," whispered Billy.

As they entered the floor of the building, it was completely dark and appeared empty. Billy stood at the door as they all filed past him, and as the last man entered, he followed him in leaving the door open behind him to shed a little light. Billy was only about three paces inside when the door slammed behind him. As he turned the whole floor lit up with builders' spotlights and they were caught like rabbits in the headlights.

In the middle of the floor, a board was standing upright. Billy tried to adjust his gaze to see what was attached to the board. As he got closer, he could hear very quiet groans, suddenly he realised that someone was nailed to the board in a crucifix position. His stomach turned as he realised it was Danny.

"Where are you?" Billy shouted.

"Nice to meet you at last Billy," Bobby said.

"Who's that?" Billy shouted back, shading his eyes against the light.

All of Bobby's men were standing behind the lights completely out of sight to Billy's gang.

"Billy, I think it's time we sorted this out once and for all," said Bobby. "Let me explain how this is going to work, I am going to shoot your dumb arse off and your men are going to watch," he continued. "Once I've finished with you, I am personally going to stick a knife through your brother's eye, so he knows how it feels. When I've finished with him all your blokes will have twenty seconds to get out of here before I start shooting them all, now is that perfectly clear?" he asked.

"Can you just run all that by me again, please?" said a voice from the shadows.

"Who the fuck is that?" shouted Bobby.

A figure appeared from behind the lights.

"Well, look who's come to join the party," said Billy, "It's DI Hobbs."

"Yes, it is Billy, now then lads I think we need a chat, I hear there is rather a lot of money at stake here," he said.

"My money," said Billy.

"I don't think so," said James coming out of the shadows alongside his brother.

"I think you'll hand it over this time," he said.

"What makes you think that?" James asked.

Billy very slowly reached into his pocket and took out his phone.

"Let me play you a recording that was sent to me earlier," he said and pressed the play button on the phone.

"Please James," the voice said, and James immediately recognised it as Lisa, "give them the money. They've found me and this time I don't think they will let me go," she said.

The recording stopped.

"So, the ball is back in my court again," said Billy.

"You can say that again," said Hobbs walking towards Billy pointing a gun at him. As he got level with him, he turned and faced James and Bobby and now pointed the gun in their direction.

"You boys should know better than to think you can cross the water and have your own way," Hobbs said, "I've been in with Billy from the start Bobby. He offered me a much larger cut than you did."

"You bastard, John," he said, "you've been playing the pair of us."

"No, Bobby, that's where you're wrong, I've been playing you all along," he told him. "Me and Billy have been working together for years," he started laughing, "you're fucked, Bobby, if we don't get the money the girl dies."

"To be honest with you I don't give a fuck about the girl," Bobby said, smiling.

"I think your brother would disagree," he said. "Anyway, let's not worry about the girl, I have two blokes sitting outside the Seaview Hotel in Torquay in police uniforms about to go in and tell your mum that something awful has happened to you two and would she mind going along with them," he looked at Bobby and smiled. "Now shall we do some business?"

Bobby could control his anger no longer, he screamed, "You total bastard," as he rushed towards Hobbs with a gun in his hand. Before he could get close Hobbs let off two rounds which hit Bobby straight in the chest and he collapsed to the floor. As James pulled his own gun, Hobbs emptied his revolver into his body.

Billy turned and stared at Hobbs.

"Why the fuck did you do that?" he screamed. "How are we going to get the money now?" he asked.

"Well, the money will have to go to either James' mum or his girlfriend, and we've got both of them." He smiled.

"John, you're a fucking genius," he said.

"Now I suggest you and your boys get the fuck out of here quickly and get Danny off that board and take him with you because my mob will be turning up soon," Hobbs said.

"What about those two?" he asked.

"Hey, you!" Hobbs shouted at Gary, who was looking very pale, "You and your mate can clear this fucking mess up, dump them somewhere where they won't be found."

"Yes, sir," Gary said.

"Everyone else out now," Hobbs ordered.

Billy and his men went out the way they had come in whilst Bobby's guys with the exception of Frank and Gary left.

They stood in silence for a moment, "Call the security guard and make sure it's all clear," Hobbs said to Gary.

Gary called the security guard. "Has everyone gone?" He asked.

"Yep, they shot out of here like lunatics," he said Gary looked over at Hobbs and nodded.

Hobbs walked over to where Bobby lay face down and just looked at him.

"I always liked you better than Billy," he said, still looking down.

"Fucking good job really otherwise you might not have put blanks in that gun!" Bobby said and rolled onto his back, laughing.

James looked across from where he was laying and smiled. "Well, I don't think the Maclarens will come looking for us again," he said, laughing.

The two brothers got to their feet, and Bobby dialled a number on his phone.

"Hi Kenny," he said, "how did it go?"

"All went well," he replied. "Lisa is on her way to the airport, and the two thugs who tried to snatch her are being taken care of," he told him, "I used a couple of mates from Leeds to get Lisa back, so they're gonna take Billy's boys out into the countryside and dump them somewhere, it'll be a couple of days before they find their way home."

"Excellent work, Kenny, Cheers mate."

"Right then you two I've got moody passports for you both and tickets to the US once you get there you can decide what to do," Hobbs told them, "and your mum is quite safe, nowhere near Torquay," he laughed.

"Me and Gary are going to drive you to Gatwick," said Frank, "Are you ready?"

"Just give me one minute," Bobby said. Then pulling Hobbs to one side, he said, "thanks for all you've done John, we couldn't have pulled this off without you."

"It was a pleasure, Bobby," he told him, "I've always hated those Maclaren bastards."

"You'll have to be careful though, if they ever catch on, they'll kill you, it goes without saying," Bobby said.

"Don't worry about me," he said, "all of the money you gave me has gone to my kids, you see I was recently diagnosed with cancer, and I've probably only got six months to live," he told him, "I'm going to retire to Spain and make the most of it."

"Shit John, I'm sorry to hear that mate," said Bobby.

"Anyway, you need to get going," Hobbs said, "Enjoy being rich." He smiled at Bobby and walked away.

The two brothers, along with Frank and Gary, headed down to the car.

"Your suitcases are in the boot," Frank said as they got in.

They drove out through South London. James was wondering if he would ever see it again. He started to go through in his mind all the things he had to do before he left. He had bought Mum a new bungalow near Margate, he had paid a nice lump of cash into Gary's account, Bobby had sorted out all his men, Geoff had received a nice lump sum in lieu of loss of earnings while the pub was being refurbished and Hobbs had been paid. That's everything done he decided.

As they drove, Gary's phone was ringing.

"Hello," he said into the receiver.

"Gary, it's Terry, is James with you?" he asked.

"Hi Terry, I'll put you on speaker," Gary said.

"Hello mate," James said, "how you doing?" he asked.

"Not very well, really," he replied.

"Why?"

"The doctors are happy with my recovery and have said I can leave the hospital," he said.

"Well that's good news, isn't it?" James asked.

"It would be, but they won't let me leave until someone pays the outstanding bill of £32,000," he said.

"Oh Shit," said James laughing. "I forgot about you, Terry, I'm sorry, I'll sort it."

"Terry," said Bobby, "You're safe there mate, stay in there one more night, and I'll have you picked up in the morning," he told him, "my man will have a passport for you and an airline ticket, get someone else to pick up your clothes from home and come and meet us in New York."

"Sounds great to me," said Terry, "I'll meet you in Manhattan."

The car pulled in to the drop off bay at the airport and Gary got out and opened the boot. As he was removing the suitcases, James gave him an envelope.

"Open it when we've gone," he told him.

James and Bobby said goodbye and went directly to the check-in area, where they found Lisa waiting for them.

"James, you are driving me fucking mad now," she said. "Lisa, I promise you it's all over," he told her, "the Maclarens think me, and Bobby are dead."

"What," she said, "why would they think that."

James told her the full story as they checked in and made their way to the departure lounge. Once in the lounge, they went directly to the bar and found Bobby and his wife opening a bottle of champagne.

As Frank pulled the car onto the motorway, Gary remembered the envelope in his pocket. He opened it and pulled out two pieces of paper. The first one was handwritten and simply said "Thanks for everything and stay safe, James." He unfolded the second piece to discover a printed remittance informing him that £1,000,000 had been deposited into his bank account. He dropped the piece of paper and sat quietly, stunned.

Frank looked across and smiled.

"The boys look after you then?" he asked.

"They most certainly did," he answered, smiling.

Billy and Jack were sitting in the portacabin in the yard.

"Well, we've seen the last of those two," Jack said.

"That's for sure," Billy answered, "now we just have to lean on the bird and the mum, and we'll have our money."

"Anyway," said Jack, "I've got to go and see Marie's family and help them with all the funeral arrangements."

"Do you want me to come with you?" Billy asked.

"No, you stay here and sort out the money," he answered as he was leaving.

Billy hadn't been able to contact the boys who had picked up Lisa, so he tried again. Once again, both phones went to answerphone. He dialled Hobbs number.

"Hobbs, its Billy," he said, "Is everything OK?" he asked "No, it's fucking not," he replied. "I've just spoken to the boys down in Torquay."

"And?" asked Billy nervously.

"She wasn't there," he said.

"What!" Billy shouted.

"She booked out this morning," Hobbs told him.

"Oh fuck," Billy said.

"Well you know where she lives, and the boys aren't around to protect her anymore," he said, "it shouldn't be a problem, and anyway you've got the girl, haven't you?"

"I can't get hold of them either," Billy said despondently.

"I'm sure they'll turn up," said Hobbs smiling, "Anyway I must rush Billy see you soon."

Hobbs hung up the phone and smiled at the young lady at the ticket desk.

"Welcome to Stanstead Airport, sir," she said, "and how can I help you?"

"I'd like a ticket for your next flight to Alicante please," he said as his smile grew.

***

James and Lisa had enjoyed two wonderful days in the Waldorf Astoria in the heart of New York and were now heading out to JFK Airport to meet Terry. As they sat in the back of the hired limousine, they watched the sights go by and chatted about the plans they would like to make for the future. As they did, Lisa held his hand very tight.

After a while, he went quiet.

"What is it?" Lisa asked.

"Well there's something I feel I need to tell you," he said.

"OK, what?"

James took a deep breath and looked Lisa directly in the eyes. "I love you," he said. It felt as though a huge weight had been lifted from his shoulders. He had wanted to tell her for so long, and finally, he'd done it.

"Oh that," she said very straight-faced, "Yes I've known that for a long time," she added. "Look we're nearly at the airport."

"What?" James exclaimed, startled.

"Were nearly at the airport," she repeated.

"But I just told you that I love you," he said. Lisa turned to look at him and started to laugh.

"If you could see the look on your face," she said and cuddling up to him whispered into his ear, "I love you too," James smiled the biggest smile of his life.

After meeting Terry and having a couple of drinks at one of the airport bars, the three of them left the terminal and returned to the limousine.

On the drive back into the city, James explained exactly how they had duped the Maclarens and made him a very generous gift for his trouble.

They pulled up outside the hotel and got out of the limousine. As they walked towards the entrance, James looked down and saw an envelope laying on the pavement as he went to pick it up, Lisa and Terry saw what he was about to do and simultaneously shouted.

"Leave it."

Chapter 25

Wednesday, 23 November 2016, New York

"Another couple of bottles of champagne please," Bobby called from the end of the bar. The Bartender smiled at him and nodded.

"No problem, sir I'll be right there," he said in his Bronx accent. The atmosphere in the bar was buzzing. It was the evening before Thanksgiving, and everyone in New York appeared to be out celebrating the fact that there was no work the following day. People entered the bar wrapped in their winter attire, blowing on their hands to try and warm them and very thankful for the heating, which made the place feel cosy. The temperature had plummeted to a mere two degrees over the last couple of days and Bobby and James Bolton were wondering why they hadn't decided to escape to somewhere with a more palatable climate. James and Lisa had kept themselves busy since their arrival in New York by visiting lots of the tourist sites whereas Bobby and his wife had spent most of their time in the Waldorf Astoria Hotel watching TV or in one of the many bars within the hotel. James could tell that his big brother was getting itchy feet. James was quite used to the quiet life and mundane days and to him and Lisa this whole experience was fantastic, and due to the lottery win, they had more money than they could possibly spend and that only added to the fun. Bobby, on the other hand, was used to being surrounded by his band of followers. Carrying out audacious raids and demanding money for protection from people who ran businesses which were not altogether honest and, therefore, couldn't go to the authorities to complain. He was already missing the life of a London villain.

They had arrived in the USA on forged passports so no check from the UK would have shown them leaving the country and the plan now was to travel to the Caribbean islands and re-enter the USA on their own passports so they could continue to live their lives as themselves. They considered that this should not be a problem as the people they were running from had seen both Bobby and James shot to death a couple of weeks ago and probably would no longer be searching for them.

The barman appeared at the end of the bar, where Bobby was waiting, carrying a tray with the two bottles of champagne and an ice bucket.

"There you go buddy," he said as he passed the tray to Bobby. Bobby thanked him and walked back to the table and put down the tray. Theresa, Bobby's wife, took a bottle from the ice bucket.

"I'll be mum," she said giggling and started to pour the drinks. "Here's to our new life in this freezing godforsaken concrete jungle called New York," she continued in a rather loud and inebriated voice. Lisa shot her a chilling look.

"We're visitors in this country," she pointed out to her, and in a whispered voice added, "and by the way, we are still travelling on forged passports and if anything happens and we get arrested we are in a lot of trouble."

"She's right," James said, "I think we should perhaps be getting back to the hotel," he added, looking directly at his elder brother.

"You guy's stay and enjoy yourselves," Bobby said, "I'll take her back and see you two in the morning."

With that Bobby got to his feet and helped his rather unsteady wife to hers after managing to get her into her coat they left the bar with Theresa still moaning about New York. A few people were looking over at the table occupied by the English tourists, which was strewn with empty champagne bottles. The barman came over and wiped up some drink that Theresa had spilt whilst trying to put her coat on and took away a couple of empty bottles.

"I am sorry about all that," James said to the bartender.

"Not a problem, sir," he replied, "is there anything else I can get you?"

"No, we're fine, thank you," Lisa replied, feeling a little embarrassed.

The bartender returned to his former position his elbow firmly planted on the bar as he leaned forward to speak to the bar owner.

"Who are the English guys," the owner asked.

"Not sure," he replied, "but their spending plenty of bucks," he said laughing, "The two who are still here are OK, but the other woman was a pain in the arse I think these two were a bit embarrassed by her."

The bar owner watched James and Lisa as they spoke quietly whilst drinking the champagne and after a few minutes he removed his rather overweight body from the stool he was perched upon and walked over to the table occupied by the English.

"Hi there," he said as he arrived at the table, "How you doing?"

"We're fine, thank you," James replied.

"I got the feeling you were perhaps a little embarrassed by your friend's little outburst," he said to them.

"Well, you know how it is," said Lisa, "Being visitors to your lovely city, it was a little out of order."

"Don't worry," he said Smiling, "My name is Joe, I own this place, and I can assure you that you are always welcome here," he said as he extended his right hand towards James. James stood and shook the man's hand.

"I'm James, and this is Lisa," he told the bar owner.

"Why don't you come and join us at the bar and have a couple of drinks on me," he said.

James and Lisa looked at each other before she turned to the man and said, "that is very kind of you, Joe, we would be delighted."

They re-camped at the bar, and Joe ordered some drinks.

"So, what brings you guys to New York then?" he asked.

"Just a bit of travelling," James said, carefully going through the story they had rehearsed in case they were asked. "Great," he replied, "where else have you been so far?" he asked.

"This is our first stop," James told him. "But we are planning on visiting some of the southern states and the Caribbean over the next couple of months."

"That sounds great," Joe said.

They sat for an hour with the bar owner discussing the differences and similarities between New York and London. He introduced them to a few of the other customers, and they were feeling very much at home by the time they decided it was time to leave. They promised to come back in again before leaving the city and left the bar.

Outside it felt even colder as they attempted to hail a cab. After a few minutes, a yellow cab pulled up beside them. "Waldorf Astoria," James said as they climbed into the back of the vehicle.

They sat and watched the people of New York scurrying around in the freezing weather coming in and out of bars and cinemas and could feel the excitement of the place. As they drove James, all singing all dancing new

American cell phone started to ring. He searched until he found the correct button and pressed it.

"James, it's Terry," the voice at the other end informed him. Terry had come over to spend a few days with them before he decided on a plan to keep himself out of the reach of the Maclaren's.

"Hi, Terry, what's up?"

"Where are you?" Terry asked.

"On our way back to the hotel," he replied.

"You better be quick," Terry told him, "I've just got back, and your brother's in reception talking to two rather angry looking coppers."

"Oh shit, we'll be there in about five minutes."

James quickly explained to Lisa what he had just been told, and her eyes rolled as she looked to the heavens. The cab pulled up outside the hotel, and as they jumped out, James threw a $20 bill at the driver. "Keep the change," he shouted from halfway across the pavement.

They entered the foyer of the hotel, and Terry came straight over to them.

"Quick their over here," he said. He turned to cross towards the reception desk with James and Lisa following behind until they reached his brother and the cops.

"Excuse me, officers," Bobby said in a very polite manner, "This is my younger brother Brian." James looked puzzled and turned to look around him for whoever Brian was, at the same time, he felt Lisa squeezing his hand. Of course, it suddenly came back to him, Brian was the name on his passport and therefore the name he had booked into the hotel under.

"Yes officer, I am Brian and Chris here is my brother," he said suddenly feeling that he was totally going over the top with the names and they would be onto him any second. "What's all this about?"

"It appears to have been a silly argument over a cab fare, but all is sorted out now," the cop told James.

"That's great," James replied.

"We will bid you a good night and a happy Thanksgiving gents," the second cop said.

As they walked away, James stared at his brother.

"What the fuck happened?" he asked.

"The bloke driving the cab took us for a pair of mugs and tried to stitch us up," he told James, "Theresa gave him a bit of lip, and the bloke got proper rude, so I told him to fuck off I took her upstairs and poured her on the bed and the next thing I knew I was getting a call from reception telling me that Old Bill wanted to see me," he continued, "so I came down, and they were here with the cab driver we sorted things out, and I paid him, and then you came in Brian," he started to laugh.

"Let's go to the bar," Terry suggested.

"Sounds good to me," Bobby said, leading the way. As they sat and had a drink, Bobby explained that as soon as they could get a flight, he and Theresa were off to the Caribbean so they could change back to their proper identities.

"I'm getting properly fucked off with all this false name shit." Bobby said.

"Me too," James agreed.

"What I'll do is once I'm back in the states I'll let you know, and you can do the same thing just in case it goes a bit tits up," Bobby said, "no point us both getting caught with the dodgy passports is there."

"No, I suppose not," James replied.

Lisa took hold of James hand under the table. "Are we going up to the room now?" she asked, smiling at him.

"Sounds good to me," James replied, standing from the table and moving her chair back so she could do the same. "See you guys in the morning," he said as he followed Lisa towards the bank of lifts situated near the reception desk.

Chapter 26

The dampness in the air only added to the atmosphere of gloom that always surrounded the day of a funeral. Many people had congregated outside the home of Marie's parents, mostly men and all wearing the traditional black tie and long black overcoat which in these parts of London is expected on such occasions. The floral tributes that had started being laid out in the front garden of the terraced house had now spilled over into the gardens either side and out onto the pavement in front of the house. The crowd stood very still making small talk and smoking as they awaited the arrival of the funeral cortege.

Everybody turned, and a silence fell over the scene as a large black Mercedes pulled up outside the house the driver jumped out of the vehicle and opened the rear passenger door, Jack Maclaren emerged from the back of the car closely followed by his brother Billy. As they walked towards the front of the house, they were joined by the third brother Peter who was accompanied by their mother. In complete silence, the four of them disappeared through the front door of Marie's parent's house.

The atmosphere within the house changed as they entered. Marie's mother had never liked Jack, and her father only put up with the relationship between them because he was frightened of Jack. They both blamed him for the death of their youngest daughter, "The car bomb was never meant to kill our Marie it was meant to kill that low life bastard Jack Maclaren," she had told people openly not caring if her words got back to him. To make matters worse for the family due to the circumstances of her death they had not been able to see her before the funeral and, in all honesty, they wondered exactly how much of her body was actually incarcerated within the coffin. Mrs Maclaren was offered a cup of tea but declined whilst the boys were all given a large shot of brandy which they drank in silence.

A member of the family came into the lounge.

"The funeral cortege is at the end of the road," he said, and everyone started making for the door. When all except for Marie's immediate family had vacated the house, Jack led his family out of the front door and along the garden pathway and waited in silence by the side of the road. Marie's family emerged from the house and came out to stand alongside the Maclaren's.

As Jack waited, he could faintly hear the sound of horses' hooves on the tarmac as the cortege approached the house. Walking proudly ahead of the horses was the Funeral Director wearing his long frock coat with Top Hat and carrying his gloves. As he arrived outside the house, he stood to one side and removed his hat and bowed as the coffin being carried on the horse carriage passed him and came to a stop. The carriage was followed by a line of six limousines all shiny black with their headlights dipped.

The Funeral Director turned to Jack and shook his hand. "So sorry for your loss Jack," the Funeral Director said, he himself was also grieving as he had known Marie since she was a young girl and had known Jack and Billy even longer. Jack put his arm around the man's shoulders and pulled him close.

"Thank you so much for all you've done," he said.

As he pulled away, Billy took the hand of the funeral director. "Thank you so much, Andy," Billy said, "you've done her proud mate."

Everyone stood and watched as the limousine drivers loaded the flowers onto all the cars and then all the passengers into the limousines. The first car carried Marie's parents and her brother and sister while Jack and his family were in the second car. The other cars were filled with more distant family members and friends. The cortege then left to make the 20-minute drive to the crematorium.

As they arrived, Jack looked out of the window and could not believe the number of people waiting for them. As he perused the crowd, he noticed almost every big-time player in the underworld was in attendance along with other cronies and hangers-on. He even noticed a few ex-coppers within the crowd.

The coffin was carried by family and friends with Billy carrying to represent the Maclaren family. The service was only twenty minutes long, but it was what she would have wanted no religion or hymns just her favourite music and tributes from her friends and family. As they all paraded out of the chapel at the end of the funeral, a queue started to form around Jack with well-wishers wanting to shake his hand and pass on their condolences. It was nearly an hour before they were back in the limousines and on their way to the reception which was being held in a hotel nearby.

Before they left the brothers took a moment to have a look at the floral tributes which had been left after they had seen them all Jack took a single rose and gave it to Marie's mother. "The flowers were lovely," Jack's mum said as they were driving away from the crematorium.

"Gorgeous," Jack said, still not feeling very talkative.

Had they looked more closely at the cards on the floral tributes they would have no doubt be puzzled by the card that simply read 'Sorry, Regards, Brian and Chris'.

Chapter 27

James and Lisa rose just before nine. Despite the weather forecast on the TV telling them that it was only going to be two degrees at its warmest today, it was gloriously sunny. After showering and dressing, they wandered down to the hotel restaurant for some breakfast.

It felt like Christmas as they came out of the lift and into the reception area. Everyone was smiling and wishing each other best wishes. As they entered the restaurant, they saw Bobby sitting alone at one of the tables.

"Morning bruv," James said as they sat at his table.

"Where's Theresa."

"Upstairs packing," he replied.

"Packing," James repeated, "Why is she packing," he asked.

"You can't get anywhere today," Lisa told him, "It's Thanksgiving you won't get a flight to the Caribbean today."

"She doesn't want to go to the Caribbean," he replied, "she wants to go home."

"Fucking hell, Bobby," said James, "She can't go home now, that could mess everything up," he continued, "Apparently the Maclarens have been snooping around your place looking for her."

"I know," said Bobby, "We've got to talk her out of it."

"Mate just tell her you're going to the Caribbean for a short holiday so you can sort the passport thing out and while you're there you can talk to her," James said.

"I can try," he answered, "I think if I can get her out of New York and this bloody freezing weather she might cheer up a bit."

A waiter appeared at the table. "Happy Thanksgiving," he said with a huge beaming smile which did little to cover up the fact that he was really pissed off because he was working while everyone else had a day off. "What can I get you?" he asked, handing out the breakfast menu.

Bobby just ordered coffee whilst James and Lisa went for the traditional pancake breakfast. The waiter scribbled a few notes on a pad and disappeared back to the kitchen with his smile still attached.

After a few minutes, the smiling waiter appeared again with coffee for them all.

They sat and further discussed the problem with Theresa and having drunk his coffee Bobby went off to their room to try and placate his extremely unhappy wife.

James had picked up a tourist guide entitled 'Thanksgiving in New York' from reception on the way to the restaurant and was now busy informing Lisa of all the fun things they could do to keep them busy all day.

"I think we should try and get a look at the parade while were here," James said, "and then perhaps Madame Tussauds later."

"At least it might be warm in there," she said, "Don't you start as well," he replied.

They finished breakfast and returned to their room for their coats and gloves. There was no sign of Bobby and Theresa, so they set off on their own. They wandered around trying to get a view of the parade only to discover that all the major vantage points were ticket only, so they headed for the waxworks. It was gone three o'clock when they returned to the hotel, and as they did, they saw Theresa standing in the reception with her cases. *This does not look good*, thought James.

"Where are you off to?" Lisa asked.

"The airport," she replied.

"And where is Bobby?" inquired James.

"He's just coming down in the lift," she said seeming happy and smiling.

"Where are you flying to?" James asked dreading the answer.

"Jamaica," she answered.

As she did the lift doors opened and Bobby appeared with a bell boy carrying the rest of the cases he looked over to James and winked.

"Can't believe we managed to get flights today to Jamaica," he told them obviously excited but probably also quite relieved due to the improvement in his wife's mood.

"I would have thought everything would be fully booked," Lisa said.

"So did we!" Theresa said, "but apparently they had a few cancellations," she said with a beaming smile, "so here we go!"

"That's great," James said, "How are you getting to the airport?" he asked.

"Taxi, I suppose," replied Bobby.

James moved closer to the reception desk and caught the eye of the young lady.

"Can I order a limousine to take my brother and his wife to the airport, please?" he asked.

"Certainly, it will be waiting outside in 15 minutes," she replied. "Don't want you falling out with any more cab drivers," James said, "have a Limo on me," he laughed.

"Well that's very kind of you little brother," Bobby said as they embraced.

Fifteen minutes later, James and Lisa stood on the steps of the hotel and waved them off in their limousine.

After spending a bit of time in their room and then going out for some dinner, James and Lisa found themselves back in the bar they had been in the night before and drinking cocktails with Joe. Before they knew it, the time had slipped by, and they returned to the hotel.

When Lisa woke the following morning, James was sitting in an armchair watching news coverage of some natural disaster. "Morning lover," she said to him smiling "Are you OK?" she asked, looking concerned.

"No, not really," he replied.

"What's the matter?"

"No wonder the airline had cancellations available for the Caribbean," he said, "it's the hurricane season."

"Oh no!" she exclaimed, "Is there one due?" she asked.

"Not due," he told her, "it hit Jamaica about three hours after they landed."

"Are they OK?"

"I don't know, I can't get hold of them," he said, "I tried the mobile and the hotel."

They both sat extremely concerned, watching the news report and waiting for updates. As James continued to watch, Lisa made them both a cup of tea and re-joined him. The news presenter was giving an update on all the reports they had received so far, as he did, he lifted his finger to his ear and held the earpiece in place while he listened to someone on the other end.

"We've just received this report from an English reporter outside the Courtleigh Hotel in Kingston," he said.

As they went to the report, Lisa looked at James. "That's where they're staying," she said.

"Yes, I know," he replied, "be quiet, I can't hear."

The reporter started describing the desolation and devastation that had been caused by hurricane 'Victor' as it ripped through the heart of Kingston during the night. He reported that most of the hotels had closed due to safety implications, and many tourists were desperately trying to make their way to the airport.

As the reporter continued to speak the camera pulled back to show some of the damage that had happened overnight, and that was when they saw them. Sitting on a bench outside the hotel, surrounded by their luggage was Theresa. Bobby was standing talking to a man and was using his hands to gesticulate something he clearly wanted to get across to him. Bobby did not look happy. The camera was on him for about thirty seconds.

"Thank God they're safe," Lisa said, looking slightly more relaxed.

"All we can do now is wait for them to get in touch with us and find out what they plan to do next," he told her.

Chapter 28

The reception after the funeral had gone reasonably well except for one incident with an uncle of Marie's who had a bit too much to drink and attempted to tell the Maclarens what he thought of them. He was as quiet as possible, ushered out of the hotel, and her family followed soon after. Once everything had quietened down Billy and Jack, who hadn't discussed business for the last couple of weeks, and a few of their closest colleagues sat at a corner table and started to discuss the events of recent weeks.

"So, what happened to the girl and their mum?" Jack asked.

"It's a fucking mystery," Billy replied, "the two guys from Leeds who were supposed to pick her up, haven't been seen since," he told Jack.

"My man up there had one phone call from them saying the girl wasn't where she was supposed to be, and It appears that they have now gone into hiding frightened because they cocked things up."

"They must have had her because they sent you that recording of her begging her boyfriend to give up the money," Jack said. "Apparently it wasn't them that sent, it" he told his brother.

"What about mum?" Jack asked, "Hobbs was supposed to be sorting that."

"Again, it's really strange," said Billy, "without anyone seeing her she apparently booked out of the hotel on the same day that Hobbs blokes were supposed to pick her up and she's never been home."

Jack looked at his brother with a puzzled expression. "We need to get hold of Hobbs again and see if he's heard anymore," Jack said.

"He has apparently retired and moved abroad," Billy informed him. "He did say that was what he would do after this job."

"So, all the money is sitting in that cunt's bank account waiting for probate to go through before anyone inherits it and we have no idea where any of their family are," Jack said, "That's fucking brilliant Billy, and you're supposed to be the brains of this outfit."

Just as the two brothers started to argue one of the other men at the table interrupted them.

"Excuse me, Billy," the man said, "but did you say that Hobbs was going to retire after this was over?"

"Yes, why?" Billy replied.

"Well, surely the plan to retire must have involved the money you were going to pay him."

"Yes, of course," Billy said, "that mug had no money saved up, he drank and gambled too much."

"OK," the man continued, "so where did he suddenly get the money from to retire?" They all went very quiet.

"That cunt stitched us up," Jack said, "I bet he did grab the mum and got the money off her."

"She wouldn't have the money yet, Jack," Billy pointed out, "as far as I'm aware they haven't even found the bodies yet."

"That's true," Jack said, "they must have hidden them fucking well," he added.

"This is all getting a bit much for me to get my head around," Billy said. "I'm getting another drink, and then I'm going home."

"We can't let this slip Billy," Jack said, "I've promised Mum we'd get her money back."

Billy rose from the table, walked to the bar and ordered himself a large Brandy. Downing it in one, he signalled to his driver that he was ready to go and left.

Billy spent the following day at the yard catching up on paperwork and making a few calls to see if anyone had heard anything about where the bodies of the Boltons had been hidden. No one knew a thing. Jack turned up about five o'clock having slept off a major hangover and again started digging Billy out about the money.

"I really don't know what to do about it," Billy told Jack, in a very resigned voice. "I thought we had everything sorted out, but it all appears to have gone tits up."

"Until they find the bodies the money isn't going anywhere, is it?" Jack said. "That's right."

"So, we need to put some pressure on to find out where they are, and then we can get somebody to accidentally find them," Jack said.

"Good luck with that," Billy said, "we don't even know who got rid of them."

"No, but DI Hobbs does, we'll have to go and find him," said Jack.

"OK," Billy said, "I know a few boys in Spain, so I'll get the word out that we're looking for him."

As they were talking, the TV was on in the background tuned into Sky TV's rolling news station. Suddenly something caught Jack's eye.

"What's that all about?" he asked Billy.

"Some hurricane in Jamaica," Billy replied, "they've been going on about it all day."

Jack grabbed the remote control of Billy's desk and pointed it at the TV. He pressed live pause and then started to rewind it. "Jack, what are you doing?" Billy asked.

"I may be going fucking mad, but I need to look at this again," Jack replied.

He pressed the button to stop the rewind and then pressed play.

"Jack, what the fuck are…"

"Shut up and watch," Jack said, interrupting his younger brother.

They both stared at the screen as a reporter was giving the details of the hurricane strike, the camera pulled back and there they were.

"Look!" Jack screamed.

"At what?" Billy asked.

"Either there is a ghost on our TV, or we've been properly turned over!" Jack shouted.

They both looked in amazement as the camera pulled in a bit closer and there was Bobby Bolton standing outside a hotel in Jamaica as large as life and with not even the slightest hint of a bullet in his chest.

"Those dirty pair of bastards!" Billy said as they both stood looking at the paused screen with Bobby looking straight back at them.

"Have you still got that bloke who works for Customs on the books?" Jack asked.

"Yes, I'll call him first thing in the morning," Billy replied.

The End